He looked up from the last bite to find Jill staring at him.

"That hit the spot," he said.

"I can tell, and you weren't kidding when you said you would eat those pancakes fast." She was obviously amused.

"Good food and good company. Nothing better after a long night."

A long, frustrating night, in this case. He hated the damn cast on his wrist and the fact he could be out of commission for weeks, if not months. He really hated that he didn't know Jill well enough to kiss her good morning. Or good night. Or all day.

Where the hell had *that* thought come from?

"I bet I know exactly what you're thinking, Houston Calloway."

Only if she could read minds, and he sure hoped she couldn't. "Huh?"

"You're lamenting the fact you're injured."

He wasn't too injured to stop fantasizing about her.

* * *

Expecting the Rancher's Baby? is part of the Texas Extreme series: Six rich and sexy cowboy brothers live—and love—to the extreme!

Dear Reader,

If you've ever watched a sporting event, you've probably noticed several people running onto the field when an athlete is injured. Among that group, you'll likely find an athletic trainer or two, and although their title might indicate otherwise, they are an integral part of the medical staff. They are charged with the responsibility of assessing injuries and rendering first aid on the field; off the field, they provide treatment and rehabilitation.

All in all, athletic trainers are the first responders and, so many times, unsung heroes. I know all this because my daughter is a superb licensed athletic trainer. And because I've rarely read a book featuring an athletic trainer, I decided to do that very thing with Jillian Amherst, an ATC who opted to join a sports-medicine team in the fast-paced and sometimes dangerous world of competitive rodeo. She is committed to providing the best care for all cowboys and cowgirls, even the uncooperative ones—like Houston Calloway.

When it comes to Jill's relationship with the stubborn bull rider, it's been strictly professional for the past two years, and somewhat contentious, to say the least. But when situations change and opportunities arise, forcing them together on a regular basis as colleagues, the sparks between them still fly, but in a completely different—and unexpected—way.

I hope you enjoy this third installment of my Texas Extreme series, and that you find it extreme Texas fun.

Happy reading!

Kristi Gold

KRISTI GOLD

EXPECTING THE RANCHER'S BABY?

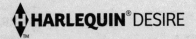

Recycling programs
for this product may
not exist in your area.

ISBN-13: 978-0-373-83871-4

Expecting the Rancher's Baby?

Printed in U.S.A.

Kristi Gold has a fondness for beaches, baseball and bridal reality shows. She firmly believes that love has remarkable healing powers, and she feels very fortunate to be able to weave stories of love and commitment. As a bestselling author, a National Readers' Choice Award winner and a three-time Romance Writers of America RITA® Award finalist, Kristi has learned that although accolades are wonderful, the most cherished rewards come from networking with readers. She can be reached through her website at kristigold.com, or through Facebook.

Books by Kristi Gold

Harlequin Desire

The Return of the Sheikh
One Night with the Sheikh
From Single Mom to Secret Heiress
The Sheikh's Son
One Hot Desert Night
The Sheikh's Secret Heir

Texas Extreme

The Rancher's Marriage Pact
An Heir for the Texan
Expecting the Rancher's Baby?

Visit her Author Profile page at Harlequin.com, or kristigold.com, for more titles.

To my daughter, Kendall—I am so proud of the woman you've become. And to my dear friend and fellow author Kathy D. for all the brainstorming on this particular book. Couldn't have done it without you...again.

Many thanks to my daughter, Kendall, MLA, ATC, LAT, for all the endless technical questions during the making of this book. Any errors in interpretation are definitely my own.

One

He wore his cowboy charisma like a practiced charmer, but the storm in his dark eyes told Jillian Amherst this rugged risk taker wasn't completely immune to pain.

When Houston Calloway strode across the first-aid tent, his black hat tipped low on his brow, the licensed athletic trainer in Jill noticed the gash in his well-worn jeans above his right knee, and that his right hand was wrapped around his left wrist below the cuff of the red shirt. Had she not been a professional, she would have only noticed his confident gait, the shading of whiskers surrounding his mouth and his above-average height. But she *was* a professional and always had been.

Besides, as a member of an elite rodeo medical

program, Jill had treated the likes of him before. In fact, she'd treated *him* before. Several times. The ever-popular rodeo superstar had enough bull-riding championship trophies to fill a football stadium and several concussions on his injury résumé. He also had a penchant for being an uncooperative patient, something she'd discovered the hard way over the past two years.

Jill rolled her chair back from the counter, swiveled completely around to face him and suppressed a frown. "What is it this time, Mr. Calloway?"

He worked his way onto the exam table across from her without an invitation. "Got my left hand caught in the rope when I was trying to get my right hand free, and I took a horn to my leg. But I made it to the buzzer."

Good for you, she thought as she stood. "Are you right-handed?"

"Yep."

"That's a plus. Any chance you fell on your head again?"

He cracked a cynical smile. "Not this time."

"That's new and different. Are you sure?"

"Yep."

Doubting she could believe him, Jill held up a finger. "Follow my movement without turning your head."

He grumbled and scowled. "I told you I didn't fall on my head. I landed square on my feet and if you don't believe me, ask Henry."

Like she'd really believe a rodeo clown wouldn't

cover for him. Jill lowered her hand in resignation, but stared at him straight on. "Okay. Fine. For now. But I'll be watching you for any latent signs. You've already had two concussions that I've treated, and who knows how many you had before that."

That earned Jill a frustrated look. "Why are you so bent on giving me grief, Jilly?"

Only one person had ever been allowed to call her by that name, and the loss of that special someone still hurt her to the core. She shook off the memories and faked a calm demeanor. "Why are you so determined to annoy me with that Jilly thing?"

He inclined his head and studied her. "It fits you better."

"Well, I don't like it and I suspect that's why you do it."

He had the gall to grin. "Would you feel better if I let you call me by a nickname?"

Jill grabbed for a little levity to defuse her frustration. "Overly confident?"

"Hmm…" He streaked his right hand over his stubbled jaw. "Overly Confident Calloway. Has a nice ring to it, but it's too long. I was thinking more along the lines of Handsome."

Shocker. "How about Crazy Calloway?"

"Been called that before. Charming?"

This exchange could go on all night if she didn't put a halt to it now. With that in mind, Jill morphed back into medical mode and turned to retrieve a pair of disposable gloves, then approached the table to inspect the cut beneath the slit in his jeans. "You're lucky. Your leg was protected from certain doom by denim. This is superficial and nothing a little antiseptic and a bandage won't cure. Now let me see your wrist."

He gingerly held the appendage out for her to examine. "Probably just a sprain," he muttered.

She pressed the fleshy part of his palm next to his thumb and immediately heard a litany of oaths. "I hate to be the bearer of bad news, but in my opinion you have a scaphoid fracture. You'll need to confirm that with an X-ray."

"I don't have time for a fracture."

She shrugged. "You're going to have to make the time if my assessment is correct."

He frowned. "How much time?"

She reached behind her, grabbed an antiseptic packet and tore it open. "That will be up to a doctor to decide."

His jaw tightened when she began to dab at the cut. "Give me a hint," he said.

After discarding the damp pad in the appropriate bin, Jill applied a plastic strip to the abrasion. "Best case scenario, three months. Worst case, six months."

Surprise passed over his expression before turning to anger. "If I'm laid up for even three months, I might as well forget making it to the finals in December."

Always chasing those championships, as were most of the cowboys who came to her for aid. "If you don't comply with any treatment you might need, you could complicate matters."

He released a rough sigh. "Can't imagine this being any more complicated than it already is."

Oh, if he only knew…and now he would. "If you go back to riding before the fracture heals, you could suffer a ruptured tendon."

"It's my left hand. All I have to do is hold it over my head to balance."

"And if you lose your balance, you risk landing on it again. I assure you that would not be pleasant."

He swiped his arm across his forehead. "None of this is pleasant."

"No, it's not, but it's unfortunately a risk you take when you climb onto a raging animal. Do you have someone who can drive you to an emergency room?"

Houston looked even more defeated. "My brother took off in the rig to hook up with some old girl-friend."

"Which one?"

He scowled. "Hell if I know who she is."

Suppressing a smile, she stripped the gloves off and tossed them into the bin behind her. "I meant which brother."

"Tyler."

Jill had treated the bronc rider once or twice, only he had always been polite and accommodat-ing, unlike his big brother. "I'm sure if you give him a call—"

"I did before my ride. He told me to find a way back to the motel and I'd see him in the morning."

"You might try calling him again."

"Did that, too. It went straight to voice mail, which means he's tied up for the night. Literally."

Clearly he'd run out of brother-based options. "Surely you can find one of your rodeo cronies to give you a ride."

He slid off the table and groaned. "I was the last entry so everyone's probably headed out. I should've done the same thing and would have if Henry hadn't convinced me to come in here to see you. I could have just as easily waited to see my doctor at home."

A new nickname for him came to mind—Foolish. "It's a long way from Fort Worth to South Texas. It's never wise to delay treatment."

"I can have my private plane here in two hours. Problem solved."

Not quite. "Sure. You could do that, and if you have any blood-flow issues, they can fit you for a prosthetic hand when you get there."

He blew out a long breath. "Since you put it that way, guess I better call a cab and get this over with, although I figure it's probably going to be a waste of time."

Jill couldn't trust he wouldn't bypass medical care and opt for the plane trip, leading her to the last resort she'd been trying to avoid. "Look, there's a satellite ER two blocks from here. You'll be in and out much faster that way, and if it's only a sprain, you can tell me 'I told you so.' I'll take you there and drop you off at your hotel after you're finished with the exam."

He seemed seriously perplexed. "Why would you do that for me?"

Her answer would reflect her strong sense of responsibility, and possibly a serious lack of wisdom. "I can report my findings to the staff while I'm there and make sure you actually go inside."

"No one waiting for you at home?"

The next response would indicate the sad state of her life. "No. Tonight I have nothing better to do aside from grabbing something to eat and settling in to my motel room. If you accept my offer, we can go as soon as I close up here."

Houston mulled that over for a moment and smiled in earnest. "Tell you what. If you'll do this for me, I'll buy you breakfast since I'm sure we won't be done before dawn."

Heavens, she hoped that wouldn't be the case. Spending all night in a waiting room as a favor for a cranky cowboy wasn't her idea of a good time.

At 5:00 a.m., with his wrist and thumb bound in a cast, Houston followed the demanding athletic trainer through the double glass doors and into the warm September night. As he trailed behind her toward the sedan, he realized he'd never observed this side of her before. He'd never really considered that she was taller than most women. He'd never seen her shiny auburn hair out of a ponytail, never noticed the way it swayed against her back when she walked. He'd sure as hell never paid much mind to how well she filled out her jeans, but then again, she was usually facing him when she tended his wounds.

But he had witnessed the impatience in her green eyes on several occasions when he'd put up a good argument as to why he didn't require her attention. He sure wouldn't mind her attention now...

Whoa, Calloway.

He had no business lusting after a member of the rodeo medical staff, even if she happened to be a really good-looking member.

Once they reached Jill's sardine-can car, Houston practically had to fold himself in half to slide into the passenger seat. Having a damn cast on his wrist didn't help much.

Jill settled behind the wheel, turned the ignition and asked, "Where to now?"

"We need to find someplace to eat."

She sent him a sideways glance. "I'm too tired to eat."

"Well, I could eat a whole side of beef. And don't forget I promised you breakfast."

"Maybe later."

For some reason he wasn't quite ready to part company with her. "I know you're itching to tell me 'I told you so,' and you can do that over a cup of coffee."

She sighed. "I've had at least four cups of coffee over the past five hours."

"That leads me to believe you won't be falling asleep soon."

She shifted slightly to face him. "You have to be the most persistent man I've ever met."

"Persistence pays off most of the time." He tried on a persuasive smile. "Come on. Join me. I promise to eat fast and talk less."

She put the car in Reverse and guided it out of the space. "Oh, all right. We can go to the diner next to my motel."

"Where are you staying?"

"The place where everyone tied to the rodeo stays," she said.

"The Buckout Inn?"

"The one and only."

He couldn't imagine her taking a room in a dive populated with crude cowboys. "That's where I'm laying over, too."

"No four-star penthouse suite?"

He stretched his legs out as far as they would go in the cramped sedan. "Nah. I'm more of a down home kinda guy."

"A down home kinda guy with a private plane."

Apparently she wasn't all that impressed. "Technically, the ranch owns the plane. I just use it now and then."

She sent him a skeptical smirk before pulling onto the street. "Ah. That explains it."

As they drove down the Fort Worth streets in silence, Houston couldn't seem to stop stealing covert glances at Jill. He took note of how well she filled out that white tailored shirt stamped with her name right above her breast. Nice, full breasts. And if she caught him staring at that immediate area, she'd probably slam on the brakes and kick his ass to the next curb. Good motivation for avoiding that. He didn't care to call a cab at the moment.

A few minutes later, they arrived at the deserted diner and claimed a booth near the window. Houston scanned the menu for a few minutes while Jill checked her cell. He raised his gaze to find her frowning.

"I'll be back in a minute," she said as she grabbed her purse, slid out of the booth and stood.

Houston figured she either planned to climb back in the car and leave him, or she needed to make a call. "Do you want me to order something for you?" he asked as she walked away.

"A glass of orange juice," she said without looking back.

Must be the phone theory, and that pleased him. He couldn't quite put his finger on it, but something about Jillian Amherst intrigued him. He decided to spend the meal trying to peg exactly what that *something* might be, provided she cooperated. First, he had to make a call, too.

After fishing his cell out of his front pocket, Houston pulled up his contacts and chose the number listed as The Tyrant. He waited through two rings before Dallas answered with, "What do you want at this time of the morning?"

"You're always up by five."

"Yeah, and Luke had us up until two."

"Sorry, but this is kind of important. I had an accident last night and—"

"Did you fall on your head again?"

"Nope. Got my hand tangled up and it's fractured, so I'm pretty much done for the next couple of months. Since I can't find Tyler, I need you to send the plane this afternoon."

"Fine, but you'll have to arrange for transportation to the airport. I'd say having you at the ranch might be a good thing, but not if you only have the use of one hand."

He started to argue that he could do more with one functioning hand than some men could do with two, but thought better of it. "It's my left hand and I can still manage."

"I damn sure hope so. And while I have you on the phone, I need to talk to you about Fort's latest demands."

Houston didn't have the time or energy to deal with Worth's twin. "Look, can it wait? I'm having breakfast with someone and she should be joining me at any minute."

"You must not be too banged up if you're with a woman."

"She's not a woman." Hell, that sounded weird. "I meant she's not a date. She's the rodeo's athletic trainer and she took me to the ER."

"Oh, yeah? How old is she?"

"Why does that matter?"

"Does she have a lot of experience in the medical field?"

"You could say that. She's tough as hell but she knows what she's doing."

"Then see if she might consider the job here."

Sleep deprivation had obviously robbed his brother of his senses. "You don't know a damn thing about her."

"Right now I'm pretty desperate. I've made a few calls but athletic trainers are in such high demand, there aren't a whole lot available around here. At least not any who are qualified to manage a program or who are willing to move to the middle of nowhere."

Houston could debate why Jill might not be a good fit, then he realized having her around wouldn't be so awful since he wouldn't be her patient, or her boss. "I'll ask, but don't get your hopes up. She seems pretty happy with her current position."

"Okay, but I expect you to use your powers of persuasion. By that I mean persuade her that it's a good opportunity without trying to seduce her. I'll have the plane there by four."

Before Houston could respond, Dallas hung up the phone in time for Jill to return to the booth, sporting black-framed glasses. "Sorry," she said. "My contacts were killing me. I had to take them off."

"You look good with glasses." And she did—smart and sexy.

She released a short laugh. "Oh, yeah. You know the old saying about women in glasses never getting passes."

"That old adage has never been in my verbal repertoire."

Her eyes went wide with surprise. "Verbal repertoire? I'm impressed."

He leaned forward and smiled. "I might look like a hayseed, but I don't just climb on the backs of cantankerous bulls. I have a degree in business with a minor in marketing."

"Really? I suppose that comes in handy with all those energy drink ads featuring your smiling face that I keep seeing everywhere."

Hell, he didn't like thinking about those, much less talking about them. "They made me an offer I couldn't refuse."

She opened the menu and turned her attention to the limited offerings. "I'm sure it helps pay the bills, like all the expenses involved in owning a private plane."

At least she'd said it with a smile. "Yeah. That, and horses and entry fees."

After setting the menu aside, she finally focused on him. "Those entry fees are pricey, especially for the cowboys just starting out. I don't know how they manage the rodeo life and a family, like many of them do."

He leaned back and sighed. "I learned a long time ago that a wife and kids and rodeos aren't a good mix. I've seen a lot of relationship casualties over the past fifteen years."

"I'm sure you have, and I assume that's why you haven't gone down that path."

"You'd be right about that." At least partially. Truth was, he'd never met anyone he'd wanted to settle down with, or anyone he'd be willing to give up the life for.

A young woman with a lopsided blond ponytail arrived at the table, set two glasses of water before them and hid a yawn behind her hand. "I'm so sorry. It's been a long night. Someone didn't show up for their shift so I pulled a double, which wouldn't be so bad if I didn't have class in four hours."

"I remember those days," Jill said. "I use to wait tables in college to avoid student loans."

"You do what you have to do to make ends meet without borrowing money," the sleepy young woman replied. "But times like these have me reconsidering."

Jill sent her a sympathetic smile. "I hear you. But rest assured it will be worth it when you don't have any debt after you get your degree."

"I hope so. Are you folks ready to order?"

"I'll just have some wheat toast and a glass of milk," Jill answered. "And some honey if you have it."

Houston frowned. "That's it? Remember, I'm buying."

"I'm a cheap date." A faint blush colored Jill's cheeks as she handed the menu to the waitress. "Not that we're on a date. And I'm not cheap. I'm just not hungry."

He chuckled. "Glad you clarified that," he said as he regarded the now smiling server. "I'll take the Western omelet with a side of pancakes and bacon. And if it's not too much trouble—" he glanced at her name tag "—Ashley, just bring me a whole pot of coffee. I'm going to need it."

The coed grinned. "No problem at all. I'll have that out shortly."

Jill took a sip of water and shifted slightly in the seat. "I hope I'm not boring you so badly that you need a whole pot of high-octane caffeine to stay awake."

Not hardly. He didn't find anything boring about her mouth or her eyes or the way she rimmed the top of her glass with one fingertip. He sure as heck didn't see anything boring about the slightly dirty thoughts that little gesture brought about. "You're not boring me at all. I've learned a lot about you in a short amount time."

She rested her elbow on the table and supported her cheek with her palm. "Such as?"

"You don't like nicknames. You don't eat enough to feed a parakeet. And you worked your way through college waiting tables, although I have a hard time picturing you slinging hash in a greasy spoon."

She straightened and smiled. "Who said I worked in a diner?"

"I just assumed—"

"Assumptions aren't always accurate. Actually, I was a cocktail waitress in a casino."

He wouldn't have guessed that in a million years. "Where?"

"Vegas, where else? That's where I discovered rodeo in relation to athletic training. I interned with my current company and that landed me a job after I received my master's degree."

And he thought nothing about her would surprise him. "Let me get this straight. You worked your way through undergraduate and graduate school by working in a casino and managed to get by without financial aid."

"I did. The money was very good. Being objectified on a nightly basis was not. But I did what I had to do to survive."

The idea of some drunk groping Jill didn't set well with Houston. He started to ask why her parents didn't help her pay for her education, but he decided that wasn't any of his business. "I admire your guts, Jill. I had no idea you could make that much serving booze. Exactly how much did you make?"

She frowned. "If you must know, on average, fifty grand a year. Some of my fellow servers made twice that much working full-time."

Damn. "I can only imagine what you went through, particularly during the rodeo finals."

Finally her features relaxed. "Nothing a good pair of glasses didn't cure."

That wouldn't have deterred him, or most of the guys he knew. "Congratulations on being resourceful, and thanks for allowing me to get to know you better."

"I know you a bit better, too."

"Oh, yeah?"

"Yeah. You want people to know you're not just a bull rider. You like the finer things in life but you downplay your wealth. You eat like a field hand and, most important, you're an incorrigible flirt."

She definitely had him dead to rights. "Am not."

"Are, too. I saw you trying your best to charm that poor, exhausted waitress with a wink and a grin."

He immediately jumped into defensive mode. "I didn't wink. I only smiled at her. In my book, that doesn't qualify as flirting. I was being polite, like my mama taught me."

She held up her hands, palms forward. "Hey, don't get your chaps in a twist. I didn't say it was a horrible trait. It's just part of your personality. Something that is second nature to you. And it's obvious you know how to contain it. You've not once ever attempted to flirt with me to get your way."

Did she want him to flirt with her? "Would it have worked?"

"Absolutely not."

Figured. "If you think about it, you've only seen me at my worst. Banged up and pissed off."

"And cranky."

He grinned. "Cranky Calloway. That's the best one so far."

They shared in a laugh until Ashley came back with the tray filled with his food and the requested pot of coffee. For the next few minutes, Jill picked at her honey-covered toast while he shoveled his food down like it might disappear. He looked up from the last bite of pancakes to find one pretty amused athletic trainer staring at him.

Houston pushed his plate away and sat back against the booth. "That hit the spot."

"I can tell, and you weren't kidding when you said you would eat fast."

The way she wet her lips brought about all kinds of questionable thoughts. "I guess you're going to tell me it's not good for digestion."

"No. I was going to say I'm glad you enjoyed it."

Her mouth held his fascination, and man, oh, man, he liked a woman with a great mouth. He also liked her slightly upturned nose and the dimples creasing her cheek, one more prominent than the other. He liked the way her slender hands moved when she spoke, and the intensity in those green eyes peering at him from behind the glasses. "Good food and good company. Nothing better after a long night." A long frustrating night, in this case. He hated the damn cast on his wrist and the fact he could be out of commission for weeks, if not months. He really hated that he didn't know her well enough to kiss her good morning. Or good night. Or all day.

Where the hell did *that* come from?

"I bet I know exactly what you're thinking, Houston Calloway."

Only if she could read minds, and he sure as heck hoped not. "Huh?"

"You're lamenting the fact you're injured."

He wasn't too injured to stop fantasizing about her. "It is what it is, and I've had worse. Dallas is going to be happy to have me home to work on Texas Extreme, although he's going to question what a one-handed cowboy can accomplish." In fact, Dallas already had.

"I'm sure you'll improvise," she said.

He could improvise when it came to her needs. Too bad he wouldn't have the opportunity to show her if Dallas offered her the job. Then again…

Houston could just hear his mom now, warning him to remember his raising and to never disrespect a woman. Unfortunately his lying, cheating dad hadn't followed that advice. He shook off those sorry memories and cleared his throat. "You're right. I'll manage."

Jill dabbed at her mouth and set the napkin aside. "Exactly what will your role be at this rodeo fantasy resort?"

"I plan to be the bull-riding instructor, as soon as I get this contraption off my wrist."

She moved her plate to one side and pushed her glasses up the bridge of her nose. "When is this venture supposed to be up and running?"

Should've been long before now. "We were supposed to be ready to go by next month, but now it looks like after the first of the year. We were warned about constructing a project this big. Expect delays and an increased budget. We've got both."

"You *are* going to have medical facilities, aren't you?"

No surprise she'd ask about that, and it was the perfect lead-in to Dallas's request. But he still wasn't sure he wanted to bother with doing Dallas's bidding. "We have a building, with nothing in it yet."

She perked up like a pup. "You should definitely utilize athletic trainers, if not full-time, on a contract basis. You'll need someone to manage that, and of course, they would also be in charge of ordering supplies, including safety gear. How close is the hospital?"

"They just built a new one off the interstate, about ten minutes or so away from the ranch."

"Excellent. You'll have an emergency room staff readily available, and you should have quick access to EMTs, just in case. Also, I suggest you might want to…"

Houston just sat back and watched Jill talk so fast he only heard half of what she was saying. He didn't like that he was starting to lust after a lady who wouldn't give him the time of day under most circumstances. More important, he hated to think he might be forced to see her on a daily basis and not be able to explore all the possibilities with her.

But that was okay. He could control himself around her if this whole employment thing came to pass.

"I'm sorry," Jill said, garnering his attention.

"Sorry for what?"

She let go a low, sexy laugh. "I'm sorry for rambling on about my ideas for your business. Once I let the passion take hold, I have a hard time stopping it."

Houston downed half a glass of water in response to the fantasies rolling around in his mind. Like *that* would help extinguish the heat building below his belt. He seriously needed to get a grip on his libido.

"Nothing wrong with being passionate about your work. It's the best way to get ahead in life. Do what you love and love what you do."

"For you that's rodeo," she stated.

"Yep. And ranching." *And making a woman feel really good all night long.*

Jill took a quick check of her watch. "Wow. It's almost dawn. Way past bedtime."

Not if he had any say-so in the matter. *Down, Houston.* "Guess that's my cue that it's time to go."

She put her palm over her mouth and yawned. "I could use some sleep, and I'm sure you should grab a few minutes before Tyler returns. Are you heading back home today?"

"Yep. I hadn't planned on it, but with a bum wrist, looks like I don't have a choice. What about you?"

"I'm laying over here until next weekend, then I'll move to a motel near Mesquite."

That meant she was free for the week, a good thing if she agreed to the interview, provided he asked her about it. Houston pulled out his wallet and tossed a fifty onto the table. "Let's go."

Jill eyed the bill for a few seconds. "Don't you need to wait for your change?"

Houston slid out of the booth and came to his feet. "Nah. She needs the money more than me."

"Very generous, Mr. Calloway," she said as she stood. "I'm sure Ashley will appreciate your contribution to the college fund."

Knowing he still had the job offer hanging over him, Houston trailed behind Jill as she headed out of the glass door and started toward the car. "I can walk from here," he told her before she climbed inside the sedan. "I could use some fresh air before I enter that musty room."

"Suit yourself," she said with a slight smile. "And if you need any advice on your medical facilities, feel free to give me a call or a text." She set her purse on the hood, pulled out a card and offered it to him. "Here you go. If I don't answer immediately, it's probably because I'm trying to put a broken cowboy back together."

He'd been that broken cowboy before, and she had always been an expert at trying to put him back together. She was an asset to the rodeo sports medicine program. She'd be an asset to any program. Hell, anyone would be lucky to have her, in a medical sense. Any other sense, for that matter.

It occurred to Houston that he wasn't quite ready to say goodbye to her yet. Not until he posed the question that could lead to a favorable response, at least for his brother, or a literal slam of the door before she drove away, leaving him to eat her dust as easily as he'd eaten breakfast. But if she agreed to consider coming to work for Texas Extreme, he could still look at her, even if he couldn't touch her. Even if he'd have to take several cold showers a day until he went back on the road. Damn Dallas for putting him in this predicament.

"Before you go, Jill," he began, "I have something else I need to say. Actually, it's an offer."

She looked more than a little leery. "What kind of offer?"

"One that I'm hoping you can't refuse."

Two

The comment robbed Jill of her speech, but only momentarily. "If you're about to proposition me, you can—"

"Do you want me to proposition you?"

She didn't intend to hesitate even a split second, but she did. "Of course not."

"Hey, relax. I have a proposition for you, but I promise it doesn't involve scooping you up and carrying you into the motel for a little predawn delight."

That stirred up a few inadvisable images in her muddled mind. "What a relief."

"Besides, that would be tough to do with my hand in a cast," he said, topping off the comment with a wily wink. He leaned back against the car, as if he had no intention of going anywhere. "First, a couple of questions."

So much for getting that snooze any time soon. "All right."

"Where is your home base?"

"Actually, I don't really have one. At least not a place of my own. I list my permanent address as my parents' house in Florida."

"You travel that much?"

"Most of the year. I live in hotels and motels and the occasional corporate apartment. I don't even own a car, so I have to rely on rentals, like that sedan you're polishing with your behind. Why?"

He shifted his weight from one leg to the other. "When you were gone earlier, I called Dallas. And when he found out you were with me, he suggested you might be a good candidate for the medical position at Texas Extreme."

That threw her for a mental loop. "He's offering me a job?"

"He wants to interview you first. It's my understanding you'd have full control over the medical program, hire anyone you want and make all the decisions."

She considered several problems with that setup and prepared to bat all his arguments away like a practiced tennis player. "Thanks, but I like the job I have."

"You'd have your own apartment. A brand-new apartment."

"I have no problem traveling. Makes life less boring."

"He'll double your salary."

He'd just served up a surprise backhand. "How can Dallas promise that if he doesn't even know how much I get paid?"

He pushed away from the car and smiled. "Doesn't matter. We can afford it."

That she didn't doubt. Still, she realized one serious obstacle remained, and she planned to lob it right to him. "No offense, Houston, but I'm not sure I could work for you."

"Not a problem. You wouldn't be working for me. You'd be working for Dallas. Besides, I'll be back on the circuit before you know it and you won't have to deal with me."

Having Houston's brother as a boss could be a major concern if Dallas Calloway happened to be as stubborn as his younger sibling. And she would still encounter Houston on a regular basis until he took off again for the next rodeo. That wouldn't be for another two to three months.

But double the salary? She'd be foolish not to give it some thought. She might be a bigger fool if she accepted without knowing all the particulars. "Look, I'd be lying if I didn't say I wasn't tempted, but—"

"I can tempt you even more."

Jill reacted to the deep grainy quality of his voice with unwelcome goose bumps. One more reason she should walk away from him and his blasted offer. Maintaining complete professionalism in his presence could be difficult outside the rodeo circuit considering his persistence, the fact that he wouldn't be her patient and this idiotic attraction to him that had begun to rear its ugly head. "I believe I have enough to make an informed decision, and my answer is—"

"A ride on a decked-out plane, complete with a fully stocked bar, in case you're nervous about flying."

"I'm not nervous." The slight tremor in her voice betrayed her, but it had nothing to do with the flight. "I can't count the times I've been on a plane."

"A private plane?"

If he only knew. "Actually, I have."

He cracked a crooked smile. "Yeah, but you haven't been on mine."

Why did everything that spilled out of his mouth sound suggestive? "And your point?"

"I just thought that since I'm done for the season, and you don't have to be anywhere until this weekend, we could mosey on down to the ranch so you can take a look around before you decide. We have plenty of places for you to stay overnight."

Overnight? No way. "I believe I've heard enough and I really don't think—"

"Pack an overnight bag, and I'll see you at four in the lobby," he said as he started across the lot toward the motel. "And FYI, I won't take no for an answer."

Wouldn't take no for an answer? Ha. Maybe that worked for most women, but Jillian Elizabeth Amherst wasn't just any woman, a fact he would soon learn. She'd spent a good deal of her adulthood telling people no, from pesky men to her own parents.

Come on, Jilly. Take a chance, for once in your life.

Jill shoved aside her onetime best friend's words and allowed caution to come into play. She had a decent life, a satisfying job. She liked the travel even if she didn't care for the solitude at times. She didn't really desire to have a permanent home or a larger salary, although she wouldn't reject extra money in most cases. But she surely didn't need the hassle of trying to avoid a cowboy who had begun to capture her fancy, and imagination. She worried she might not *want* to turn him down, if the opportunity presented itself.

That reason alone led her to the appropriate decision. When Houston Calloway walked into that lobby this afternoon, he wouldn't find her there.

Houston was kind of surprised to see Jill standing there, a blue canvas bag hanging over her shoulder, a larger suitcase at her feet and a ticked-off look on her face. She struck him as one of those organized people, and she probably didn't appreciate the fact he was ten minutes late for the rendezvous.

"Not much on punctuality?" she said as he approached her, confirming his suspicions.

"Sorry," he muttered. "I overslept."

"I didn't sleep at all."

She'd said it like that was his fault. "Why not?"

"Aside from having to turn in my rental car, I kept

rolling your offer around in my mind, weighing the pros and cons. Instant insomnia."

No shock there. "Fair enough. Now follow me."

After picking up her suitcase, Houston escorted Jill out of the lobby to the black limo waiting at the curb. The driver opened the rear door and took the suitcase while Jill climbed inside. She claimed a spot on the lengthy seat on the far side of the limo, while he sat opposite her to maintain a wide berth between them. Otherwise he'd be battling the urge to coax her down onto the gray leather.

Like she'd be open to that. And he sure as hell didn't understand why he'd suddenly become so damn attracted to a woman who'd been a burr in his butt for two years. Maybe it was just the challenge and the chase. Maybe he'd gone too long without female attention. Maybe it was those dimples and that shiny auburn hair and the way that peach-colored T-shirt enhanced her finer attributes. And damn she smelled good, like the lavender his stepmom, Jen, planted everywhere she could find a scrap of dirt. Jillian's finer qualities, coupled with her no-BS attitude, presented a mighty fine package. He could so take her on one, hot ride…

"Nice ride," she said, breaking through his fantasies.

"Only the best. The bar's fully stocked if you want a drink."

"No, thanks. When I drink, which is extremely rare, I don't ever do so before seven."

He could use a shot of whiskey, but he'd refrain in

order to maintain some control over his libido. "Did you have any lunch?"

"I grabbed a sandwich a couple of hours ago."

When she flipped that thick hair over one shoulder, he wanted to grab a cab and get out of there before he forgot his manners. "We'll have dinner with the family tonight," he said. "That would be a welcome change of pace. I tend to have a lot of fast food."

"I hear you. Nothing better than a home-cooked meal."

"I agree," she said before glancing out the window.

Houston still couldn't quite get a grip on the fact she'd agreed to accompany him in light of all her earlier arguments against it. He sensed Jill might be questioning that decision when she shifted and turned her attention onto the smoky glass partition separating the front from the back. The conversation died during the twenty-minute drive to the private airport and didn't resume even when they boarded the D Bar C corporate jet.

They settled into the beige leather seats kitty-corner from each other in the main cabin near the onboard bar. Jill stared out the window without speaking, leading Houston to wonder why she would find a hangar so damn interesting.

He snapped his seat belt closed and cleared his throat. "How does this plane compare to the others you've been on?"

She tore her gaze from the tarmac and looked

around. "About the same," she said before finally looking directly at him. "Plush seats. Full kitchen with white marble counters. The ultimate in technology, right down to the WiFi. I assume the sleeping quarters are in the back."

"Yeah. Feel free to stretch out after we take off."

She rifled through her bag, took out a magazine and began to flip through the pages. "No, thanks. I'm fine right here."

All talk ceased as they taxied down the runway, and once they leveled off midair, Houston got up and grabbed a beer from the bar fridge. "Want anything to drink? I make a mean gin and tonic."

"No, thanks," she said without looking up.

"Glass of water?"

"No, thanks again."

Jill seemed bent on ignoring him, and that royally ticked Houston off. He took a swig before settling back in the seat. "Did I do something to piss you off?"

She sent him a fast glance and went back to flipping. "Not today."

"What is that supposed to mean?"

After closing the magazine, she looked at him straight on. "I'm sorry. I'm tired. I didn't intend to take it out on you."

He suspected there was more to it than fatigue. "Are you sure something else isn't bugging you?"

"If you must know, my mother left me a voice mail and I listened to it right before I left the motel room. She reminded me that my sister is getting married next weekend and I'm expected to attend. Sometimes her demands rub me the wrong way."

Houston decided Ms. Amherst had some serious mama issues. "You don't sound too excited about the nuptials."

"I'm not. I've never been that close to Pamela. She'd didn't even invite me to be in the wedding party. But I'm five years older and let's just say she's always been the favored child."

He sensed a sorry story there. "Why is that?"

"Pamela is a conformist. She went to college at my parents' Ivy League alma mater, and she had the good fortune to find the perfect, wealthy, shallow guy. I'm sure she'll go on to be surrounded by lots of socialites and have two point five children and a membership to the best country club in the country."

. The resentment in her tone took him aback. "Not your scene, huh?"

"Not hardly. I'm the rebel of the family. I went to school in Sin City and didn't take the time to meet any guys, let alone get engaged to one."

That was one helluva bombshell. "You didn't date a single soul in college?"

"I was focused on my career, although I did consider seeking out a professional poker player just to add fuel to the family fire."

They both laughed for a few seconds before Houston posed another question to keep the mood light. "Don't you think bringing home a cowboy would've done the same thing?"

She mulled that over for a moment. "I wish I'd

thought of that. My mother would have been completely beside herself, but at least she might have stopped trying to set me up with some rich, boring, misogynistic narcissist every time I went home."

Man, she didn't mince words. Big words. But he'd started to relate a little more to the always serious athletic trainer. He wasn't a stranger to complicated family dynamics, and he was curious to confirm if they shared another aspect in their background. "Correct me if I'm wrong, but it sounds to me like you come from money."

She folded her arms beneath her breasts and sighed. "Yes. A lot of money. I had a trust fund that I didn't bother to touch because it came with conditions."

That explained why she worked her way through school. "Conditions as in Ivy League schools and no cowboys?"

"Exactly."

A short span of silence passed before Houston decided to end the quiet for a second time. "I'm glad you let me in on the family problems. For a minute there I thought you were mad at me for forcing you onto a plane."

Her smile came back out of hiding. "You didn't force me, and no, I'm not mad at you. I *am* a little mad at myself for not declining the invitation. This could be a total waste of both our time if your brother isn't interested in hiring me. Provided I actually want the job."

"Or it could be a win-win situation. You'll have a

better salary and a permanent place to land, and I'll earn some points with Dallas."

She frowned. "Are you holding some sort of competition?"

"Yeah. See who can find the prettiest prospective employee."

"That's rather sexist, Calloway."

"I'm kidding, Amherst. Dallas thinks I haven't been doing enough for Texas Extreme, so I figure finding someone as qualified as you to head the medical team will help prove my worth."

"Ah. Now I know your true motives. I could be a notch in your bedpost. I meant notch in your belt buckle. Or is it just belt? Never mind." Her face looked a little flushed. "What is Dallas like?"

"I thought you'd probably met him."

She shook her head. "No, but I do know his reputation as an all-around champion cowboy."

"Do you know Austin?"

"Again, only by reputation. I did catch a glimpse of him during the national finals when I was interning, but I never had the chance to meet him."

"Is that his rodeo reputation or his reputation with the ladies before he got hitched?"

"His rodeo reputation. With you, I'd say both."

Ouch. "Aw, come on now. I'm not a player."

She narrowed her eyes and smirked. "That's not what I've heard."

"You can't believe everything you hear in the rodeo world. People like to exaggerate."

"I'm sure."

He didn't care for her cynical tone, or that she believed he was some skirt-chasing cowboy. That would be his half brother Worth, and the minute she met him, she might change her tune. Compared to Worth, he'd look like a saint. "To set the record straight, I had a girlfriend for a couple of years."

She leaned back and crossed her jeans-covered legs. "Really? What happened to the relationship, if you don't mind my asking?"

He did mind a little bit. "She got tired of me being gone all the time."

"She wasn't into rodeo?"

"Nope. She was a city girl from Dallas. She lived in a downtown loft and unfortunately tennis was her sport."

Her green eyes went wide. "Unfortunately? What's wrong with tennis?"

Open mouth, insert boot. "I take it you play."

"Yes, but not much since my boarding school days."

That nearly shocked him speechless. His family had always been well off, but they'd never shipped him off. "Like a live-in school?"

Jill looked like she wished she could take it back. "Yes. All-girl college prep academy, thanks to my mother's insistence. I concentrated on my studies, and not on boys."

He'd begun to wonder if she'd never had any exposure to the opposite sex. Nah. Not possible with her looks and smarts. "Surely you had a boyfriend at some point in time."

The way she lowered her eyes for a second told Houston he might already know the answer. "I've dated a little," she finally said. "But with my bachelor's degree, grad school, internships and a demanding job, my schedule hasn't allowed for much of a social life for the past few years."

He'd be glad to help her change that, but she probably wouldn't be game. Then again, if it didn't work out between them and she did go to work for the ranch, that could cause a lot of issues. "I imagine it would be pretty hard to have much of a social life with all the traveling, particularly in your line of work."

"Most men don't seem to have that problem."

He couldn't resist yanking her chain. "Isn't that a little sexist?"

She rolled her eyes and smiled. "Oh, please. That's the way it is. Men have an uncanny way of finding a woman in every port. Or in your case, arena."

"You're jaded."

"I am not. I only tell it like it is."

"Nope. You've been wronged by someone, most likely a cowboy."

She raised her hand like she was taking an oath. "I swear I have never been involved with a cowboy. I *have* been a silent observer during my tenure as an athletic trainer and I've seen it all. Broken hearts. Heated arguments. I've even treated the casualties resulting from cat fights."

He chuckled. "Gotta love those cowgirls."

"Let me add that I've also examined more than a

few jaws resulting from cowboy fights, even if that's not in my job description."

"But not with me."

She grinned again. "No, not you. You're more inclined to fall on your head when you fall off a bull and then argue with me when you don't want to hear my advice."

He studied her a moment and had a surprising revelation. "I've got to be honest with you, Jill. When I first met you, I didn't like you much."

She laid a hand above her breasts. "I'm stunned."

"That's sarcasm, right?"

"Yes. You didn't like it when I ran you through concussion protocol."

"True. And I didn't particularly like that you seemed to treat other cowboys nicer." Now he sounded like some jealous jerk.

"You don't like anyone telling you what to do," she began, "and most of my patients tend to be much more cooperative."

Damn if she wasn't right about that. "Fair enough. But you tend to make a big deal over a bump on the head, at least when it comes to me."

She unbuckled her seat belt and scooted forward, her hands clasped together in her lap. "Look, Houston, I'm only tough because I care."

"You do? Well, ma'am, I'm mighty honored to know that."

"I care about every athlete I treat," she added quickly.

"Even the annoying ones?"

Her smile traveled all the way to those great green eyes. "Yes, even the annoying ones."

When Jill yawned, Houston realized he was being selfish by keeping her from sleeping. "Are you sure you don't want to go to bed?"

"We don't know each other *that* well."

Finally, another glimpse of her sense of humor, although he didn't find the stirring below his belt funny at all. His "bed" question might've been totally innocent, but the images hanging out in his head were pretty damn wicked. "You know what I mean. You're about to fall asleep where you sit, which you can. Just press the button on the right side and the chair leans all the way back."

She blinked twice. "I'm fine. Really."

"You can barely keep your eyes open." He stood, stepped to one side of her seat and depressed the control, reclining the back of the chair and raising the foot rest at the same time since she refused to do it herself. "There you go."

He expected her to protest, but instead she muttered, "Thank you."

For some reason, Houston's feet remained glued to the floor as he continued to hover above Jill, leaving them in close proximity. She wet her lips and looked like she might want to say something, or do something, but she just sat very still, her gaze locked on his. He seriously wanted to kiss her, long and hard, but his mom's words about honor kept him from acting on impulse. Jill had been right. They didn't know each other that well, but if he had his way, that would change, if only to find out if his attraction to her was legitimate. He probably wouldn't get his way, so he should just stop thinking about that now.

"Have a nice nap," he said as he moved back to his seat.

"I will," she answered before closing her eyes completely.

Houston downed the rest of his now-warm beer and continued to watch Jill. He knew by the rise and fall of her chest, her slack features, she was out. She was also a pretty sleeper. Angelic. Sexy. So much for not thinking of her in that way.

He rested his head back against the seat and allowed his imagination free rein, at his own detriment. Every detailed fantasy made him more uncomfortable. Every questionable thought about what he wanted to do with her made him shift on the seat. And every time he tried to stop thinking about it, he met mental resistance head-on.

If he didn't get hold of his control, by the time they made it to the ranch, he'd have to ride in the pickup bed.

Bed.

Damn. Asking Jill Amherst on this trip was definitely asking for trouble.

Three

"Buckle up, folks. We're about to land."

At the sound of the booming voice, Jill came awake with a start. She looked around to try to regain her bearings, and came in visual contact with a pair of golden-brown eyes. Now she remembered. Private jet. Persistent cowboy. Possible new employment.

She stretched her arms above her head and made sure her seat belt was secure as they started to descend. "How long have I been asleep?"

"Less than an hour," Houston said. "It's a fairly short flight."

As she braced for landing, Jill glanced out the window to see the roofs of several houses with pools and huge barns, and on the horizon, a huge multistory building surrounded by a massive amount of acreage. "Where are we landing?"

"The ranch. We have our own airstrip."

Of course. "It looks like suburbia in the middle of nowhere."

"We've all built our own houses, so I guess it would look that way. People in these parts like to refer to the D Bar C as the Cowboy Commune."

She brought her attention back to Houston. "Clever. I look forward to seeing the commune up close and personal."

The tires bumped and the plane screeched to a halt, followed by a resounding "Yee haw" coming from the vicinity of the cockpit.

"Who in the world was that?" she asked.

"That's Frank, the wannabe cowboy pilot," Houston said. "I forgot to warn you about him."

She wondered what other surprises awaited her. "I appreciate his enthusiasm." And she was happy that she hadn't been bucked out of the airplane.

After releasing her seat belt, Jill grabbed her bag and stood. Houston followed suit, but before she could take a step toward the exit, he said, "Just so you know, my family's kind of unconventional."

She would save that conversation for later. "Not a problem. You should meet mine."

Without waiting for a response, Jill headed out the now open door and sprinted down the stairs into the very warm Texas evening, Houston following behind her. She spotted a huge, black double-cab truck parked across the airstrip, a red Texas Extreme logo emblazoned across the side. And leaning against that truck, a guy with ham-hock biceps and sun-streaked hair. He wore a lemon yellow T and jeans and aside from the worn cowboy boots, he looked a bit out of place against the rustic backdrop.

The minute they made eye contact, he looked somewhat surprised to see her. Not as surprised as she was to see the likes of him on a ranch—a surfer dude. Definitely not the typical rodeo guy, which led her to believe he must be either a friend or employee of the Calloway boys.

"Hey, brother," the stranger said as he pushed off the truck.

Brother? Seriously? A brother with a serious air of confidence, Jill decided when he strode toward them, all the while keeping his gaze trained on her.

"Hey," Houston replied as he took the bags from the rowdy pilot with the handlebar mustache, who looked more like a gunslinger than an aviator. "Jill, this is Worth, the youngest of the crew."

"I'm a minute older than Fort," Worth said with a frown. "That makes me second to the youngest, and it's nice to meet you, Jill."

She'd known about Dallas, Austin and Tyler, but Fort and Worth had never entered any conversation she'd had about the Calloways. "Nice to meet you, too."

Worth sent her a slow grin. "I didn't know you were bringing a girl home, Houston."

Houston shoved a black canvas bag at Worth. "She's not with me, and she's not a girl."

"Okay, she's a woman and I saw her get off the plane with you."

"Yeah, but she's here to see Dallas about a job."

Worth turned his smile on Jill. "How long are you going to be here?"

She sensed the man was an incorrigible flirt. "Only one night."

"Would you like to go with me to—"

"No, she wouldn't, Worthless," Houston snapped. "Take our bags to my house. And tell Mom to set an extra plate for dinner."

Worth looked as confused as Jill felt. "I'll drive you to your place."

After handing over a set of keys to his brother, Houston picked up Jill's luggage and started toward the truck. "We'll walk," he said as he put the bags in the bed.

Worth saluted. "Aye, aye, captain. I live to serve."

After Worth climbed back into the truck and drove away in a fog of dust, Houston turned to Jill. "I want to apologize for his behavior. He only has two things on his mind—women and chasing women."

Information she'd already gathered herself. "He seemed nice enough."

"He's a twenty-seven-year-old teenager."

"A year older than me," she said without much thought.

"Maybe chronologically, but not on a maturity level."

"Does he work here on the ranch?"

"Yeah, but he owns a yacht-chartering company on the gulf coast."

That explained the surfer look. "And apparently he has a twin."

"Yep. Fort, but he doesn't have anything to do with any of us."

Interesting. "Why is that?"

"It's a long story."

One she might never know. She did have an important question involving the rest of the family. "When you asked Worth to tell your mother to set an extra plate, it made me wonder if anyone knows I'm here."

He looked a little sheepish. "Only Dallas, but the rest will real soon, now that Worth knows."

"I don't want to inconvenience anyone."

"It's not a big deal," he said. "We have guests dropping by all the time.

Now follow me and I'll show you around."

"I'm looking forward to it." She wasn't exactly sure how she felt about being the surprise for the evening, or staying in Houston's house, but then again, it shouldn't matter. She was here on business, and she'd established that from the beginning. She didn't believe that Houston was the kind of guy who had to be reminded of that. Besides, he'd never held her in high esteem, although he had thought enough of her to present what could be a great opportunity. Provided she got past the initial first impressions. She had a feeling this could be an interview by committee.

They continued down a narrow paved road while

Houston pointed out various landmarks, including the massive lodge in the distance, the new rodeo arena, complete with indoor and outdoor space. Then he pointed at the rock and cedar building adjacent to those facilities. "That's the medical clinic. I'll take you on a tour after dinner."

Clinic? She'd been expecting a glorified tent. "I'm pleasantly surprised. It looks top-grade."

"Right now it's empty," he said. "That's where you come in."

"If Dallas thinks I'm the right fit."

"He will."

Confident much? "*If* I decide it's something I want to undertake."

He grinned. "You will."

She'd learned from experience that debating with Houston Calloway would do no good, so Jill concentrated on meeting him stride for stride as they took a left turn at a bend in the road. The first of the residences came into view, a white rock and cedar single-story rambling ranch house set back from the road on their right. From the looks of the place, she guessed this place belonged to a matriarch, until Houston said, "This one's mine," shattering all her assumptions.

"Wow," she said as they headed up the driveway toward the three-car garage. She took note of the silver crew-cab truck, the typical rodeo cowboy's mode of transportation. Admittedly she was a little stunned to see the champagne-colored Mercedes parked next to it.

"Great," Houston muttered. "We have a guest."

"Old girlfriend?"

"Nope. New stepmom. That's her car."

"Worth's mother?"

"Yeah. Jenny. I've got to warn you, she's one of a kind."

"In a good way?"

"Most of the time."

Jill wasn't sure how to take that until the door opened to a woman with teased blond hair and a sunny smile. She wore a red polka-dot dress, covered by a white frilly apron that looked like a throwback from fifty years ago.

"Come in," she said with a sweeping gesture. "We're so glad to finally meet one of Houston's special friends."

"She's not a special friend," Houston corrected as they stepped inside the entry. "She's a prospective employee."

"Whatever you say." She turned her attention to Jill. "I'm Jenny, Houston's stepmama. And you are?"

Jill shook her offered hand. "I'm Jillian Amherst, but most people call me Jill."

"What a lovely name," Jen said. "For a lovely girl."

"No offense, Jen," Houston began, "but what are you doing here?"

"No offense taken, sugar. When Worth told me you'd brought home a guest, we decided to bring dinner home to you. Dallas, Paris and the baby are on their way. Now Austin and Georgie might be along a little later because Chance just took a tumble off the fence."

Jill immediately launched into medical mode. "Is he all right?"

Jen waved a dismissive hand. "Oh, certainly, sweetie. This is a daily occurrence with that seven-year-old. He's a walking accident waiting to happen."

Houston finally closed the door behind him. "How long until dinner?"

"That depends on how long it takes you to fire up the grill," Jen said.

Houston's expression turned stony. "We're having a barbecue?"

Jen looked at him as if he'd grown a second eye. "Of course. It's Labor Day weekend, sugar. I brought the burgers and all the fixins' plus a few hot dogs. I even have one of those fake patties for Paris. Your mama will be here in a bit with the apple pie."

Funny, Jill hadn't given much thought to the holiday. In fact, she hadn't remembered the date when it came right down to it. "That sounds great. I'm on the road so much, I can't remember the last time I celebrated a holiday."

"Well, that ends today." Jenny waved Jill toward the lengthy hallway to the right. "I'll show you to your room while Houston gets after that grill. Otherwise, we won't be eating until midnight."

As the enthusiastic stepmother began leading her away, Jill shot a glance over her shoulder at Houston. He sent her a sympathetic look before disappearing from the foyer.

So much for being rescued, Jill thought as she followed Jenny down the corridor, which seemed to run the length of the house.

Jenny paused at the end of the hall and opened a door. "Here we are. Your accommodations for the evening."

Jill walked into the tastefully appointed room to find her bags waiting at the foot of the queen-size bed covered in a rich purple satin comforter. She didn't peg Houston as a purple kind of guy, but then she doubted he had anything to do with the decor.

"I decorated this room," Jenny said, upholding Jill's conjecture. "In fact, I decorated all the boys' places, otherwise they'd be covered in cowhide and wood."

"You did a great job."

"Just wait till you see the bathroom," Jenny said as she practically skipped across the room to open another closed door.

Jill came up beside her and peered inside to see a white Cararra marble tile shower with matching countertops on the vanity. As impressive as it was, she had to admit it looked a lot like other bathrooms she'd known in her lifetime.

Determined not to disappoint Jenny, Jill turned and smiled. "It's very beautiful. I'm extremely impressed by your eye for decorating."

"Oh, thank you, sugar. Now before we go back out into the crowd, we need to have a little chat."

She could only imagine what that might entail. "Go ahead."

"First of all, you need to know you're going to be immersed in testosterone tonight. The Calloway men are a virile bunch. They can hang their jeans on the bedpost and get a woman pregnant."

That created quite a visual in Jill's mind. "Believe me, I deal with that every day in my job. Not the jeans thing, but the testosterone."

"Well, just so you're forewarned." Jenny grinned. "I can't wait for you to meet Paris and Dallas. You know, Paris worked for Dallas in exchange for marrying him."

Jill would swear she'd read that scandalous novel before, and although she wished she had more details, she decided not to prod. "Interesting."

Jenny sighed. "Oh, sweetie, it was. But then they fell in love, married and had a precious little boy eight months ago."

"What a wonderful story."

"And when it comes to Austin and Georgie, that was a love story decades in the making. They were high school sweethearts torn apart by family feuding and unavoidable circumstances."

"Obviously it all worked out."

"Yes, but not before they reunited for one magical night and conceived Chance. Of course, Austin didn't know about him for a good six years."

She'd read that book, too. "That must have been quite the bombshell."

"It almost tore them apart for good. Thankfully we banded together and talked some sense into the boy. And now they're living in wedded bliss as Romeo and Juliet, without the poison and dagger."

Jill was suffering from serious information overload. "I can't wait to meet them all, too."

Jenny hooked her arm through Jill's. "Then let's get to it."

Jill pondered what she'd gotten herself into. Correction. What she might be getting into if they came to an employment agreement. Right now she only worried about getting through the introductions.

They made their way through the masculine great room, complete with black leather sofas and, unsurprisingly, cowhide chairs as well as a large stacked-stone fireplace grounding the room. The kitchen was all Jill expected—high-end appliances, concrete countertops and a butcher-block island the size of Rhode Island. She wouldn't be a bit surprised to see a butler. Oh, wait. That would be her family home.

"Just go on out back, sugar," Jenny said as she opened the huge stainless refrigerator. "I'm going to season the burgers and I'll join you in a few with some of my special drinks."

"Sounds great."

After walking through a set of French doors, Jill entered a backyard that could best be described as resort-like, right down to the pergola and the pool. She found Houston lighting the grill built into a second kitchen built out of stone, a barbecue master's dream.

When Houston glanced at her over one shoulder, he smiled slightly. "Did Jen give you the grand tour?"

She pulled back a cushioned wicker chair from

the round glass table nearby. "Yes, she did. She also gave me a recap of your brothers' love stories."

He lowered the lid on the grill and faced her. "I can only imagine what she said."

"Let's just say it was enlightening."

"No surprise there. Where is she now?"

"She's getting the burgers ready and making some kind of special drink."

Houston raked back the chair across from her and sat. "I have to warn you about that. Drink it slow and don't have more than one."

"Does she add something else?"

"Yeah. Tequila."

She'd expected maybe some sort of fruit. "I took a few tequila shots once back during my college days."

"Did you enjoy it?"

She grinned. "I don't remember."

"I've had a few of those nights."

"That was my one and only. I'm too much of a control freak to get drunk."

"Sometimes letting go of a little control is a good thing."

She rested her elbow on the table and supported her face with her palm. "Not when it comes to booze."

"Maybe I wasn't referring to booze."

Normally she would ignore the comment, but for some reason she had to ask. "Care to cite some examples?"

He leaned back and smiled. "Sometimes it's better

to take a few risks. Follow instinct instead of logic. Do what feels good."

The overt sensuality in his tone drew her in like he was a human magnet and she was steel. "But what if feeling good in the moment leads to regret later?"

He leaned forward and kept his gaze trained on hers. "Life sometimes comes with regrets, but if you don't take a chance now and then, you're not really living."

Maybe he was talking about the job opportunity. Maybe he'd been speaking in generalities. Maybe she should move on and change the subject. "Just don't expect me to ever climb on the back of a bull."

"Nothing better than a good, long ride."

"I'd never last for the required eight seconds."

"Darlin', I've been known to go way past that."

"Really now?"

"Really. You just hang on tight, tune into your body and roll with the flow."

Oh, heavens. The images his words conjured up would make a Vegas showgirl blush. Images of tangled limbs and bare flesh and…

She didn't flirt. She didn't lust. Never. Okay, almost never. But Houston had an uncanny knack for making her fantasize about things she shouldn't even be considering. After all, he'd been a patient less than twenty-four hours ago.

Her attention went straight to his bandaged hand as a reminder, yet the thought of his good hand on her…

Jill brought her focus back to Houston's face and

he sent her a knowing smile. She found herself smiling back and wondering what would happen next when he stood and rounded the table. He stared down on her a few moments before he braced his hand on the back of her chair, lowered his lips to her ear and whispered, "Just let me know if you want to take a chance and take that ride."

She shivered slightly before she snapped back into reality. Two could play this game. *Don't count on it*, she intended to say. "Are you sure you can handle me?" came out of her mouth. Apparently he had channeled her inner vixen and she hadn't even known she had one.

He grinned again. "I'm up for the challenge."

Before she could respond, an attractive blonde woman stepped out the patio doors, a precious sandy-haired baby on her hip and a tall, handsome man following behind her.

"Hi, Houston," the woman said. "Dallas told me about your poor hand. Does it hurt much?"

"Naw." Houston held up the cast. "It's going to come in handy when I need to hitchhike."

"It's not going to come in handy when you have to do some work around here," the presumed brother muttered.

Houston turned back to Jill. "This is Dallas and his wife, Paris," Houston said. "This is Jillian Amherst."

Jill popped out of her seat like someone had lit her bottom on fire and worried she might looked guilty, as if she'd been caught doing something nefarious with Houston. "It's nice to finally meet you both."

Dallas stuck out his hand for a shake. "Good to meet you, too."

Paris smiled and said, "Welcome to the zoo and this is our little monkey."

"He's also known as Luke," Dallas added.

Clearly the Calloways had run out of Texas city names for the next generation, unless…

"In case you're wondering," Paris began, "it's not short for Luckenbach."

At least that answered Jill's question. "He's a handsome little guy. How old is he?"

"He'll be nine months on October first. I won't be a bit surprised if he's walking before then."

"Neither will I," Jenny said as she breezed onto the patio with a tray of amber-colored drinks and bowls filled with salsa and chips. "Thought you might all like to have some appetizers and drinks before dinner."

"I think I'll have a beer," Houston said. "Otherwise I might burn the burgers."

"Luke is still nursing," Paris began, "so I'll have to pass."

"A beer sounds good to me," Dallas chimed in.

Jenny leveled her gaze on Jill. "Surely you'll try one of my famous mint juleps, sugar."

Refusing the offer would simply be rude. "Of course."

While everyone stood there and watched, Jill took one tumbler and sipped some of the concoc-

tion. She should have known by the smell alone that
the drink would curl her toes. And her board-straight
hair. When her eyes began to tear, the crowd began
to laugh. Most of them.

Jenny frowned before she turned her smile on Jill.
"You'll get used to it, honey. By the third or fourth
swallow you'll be clamoring for another one."

Most likely she'd be passed out under the table.
"I do like the fresh mint. It tempers the alcohol."

Jenny patted her cheek. "Spoken like a true South-
erner. Are you from the South, sugar?"

"Nothern Florida," she answered around the burning in her throat.

"Why, that's Southern enough in my book."

The door opened again, this time to a petite olive-
skinned woman with long dark hair, and at her side,
a little boy she couldn't deny. "Sorry we're late," she
said. "Chance decided to take a dive off the fence."

"I didn't dive, Mama. I fell off a little."

She ruffled his thick dark hair. "You scared the
heck out of me."

"Where's Austin?" Houston asked.

"Unsaddling the horse. He'll be along in a minute." She eyed Jill for a few seconds before she spoke
again. "Hi. I'm Georgie, Austin's wife, and you are?"

"I'm Jill." She still remembered her name, a good
thing.

"Jill Amherst," Houston added. "She's here to talk
to Dallas about the medical job."

Georgie eyed the glass still clutched in Jill's hand.

"And you decided to get her drunk with one of Jenny's drinks before the interview?"

"Oh, hush now, Georgia May," Jenny scolded. "Now why don't you and Paris and the kiddos join me in the kitchen while these three talk business?"

"Good idea," Paris said. "This little guy is getting heavy. Is your kitchen child-proof, Houston?"

Houston scowled. "What do you think?"

"Probably not," Paris said. "I'll just keep him away from all your pots and pans."

Once the women filed out, Jill was more than happy to be seated again, although she found herself taking another drink of the julep. Then another. Nerves, she supposed. And not very wise.

She slid the glass to one side and prepared for Dallas Calloway's inquisition, when Paris emerged from the house holding two beers that she placed on the table.

"Here you go," she said, then patted her husband's back and kissed his cheek. "Go easy on her, okay?"

Dallas smiled up at Paris. "If she can survive Jen's drink, she can handle a few questions."

Jill wasn't so sure about that, especially when Houston got up from the table. "Since this is Dallas's thing, I'm going to feed my horse real quick before I have to go back to grill duty. And, Dallas, like your wife said, cut her some slack."

Dallas frowned. "To hear you two tell it, I'm some kind of a jackass."

Houston grinned at Jill. "There's only one kind, brother."

With that, he walked back into the house, leaving Jill alone with a virtual stranger. She wasn't too crazy about the abandonment, and when Dallas trained his blue eyes on her in a serious stare, something suddenly dawned on her. A temporary escape to gather her wits. "I should probably retrieve my résumé. It's in the guest room."

"No need for that," Dallas said. "Let's just keep this casual."

Casual she could handle. "Sounds good. What would you like to know about me?"

"Ever worked around horses?"

That she didn't expect. "Actually, I used to ride when I was younger. Competitively, but it's been a long time." Yet it seemed like yesterday when the accident that claimed her best friend had caused her to quit.

"What did you compete in?"

"Hunter and jumper competitions."

"Does Houston know this?"

"No. Why would he?"

"When he mentioned you might be interested in the job, he told me you'd known each other for a couple of years."

"We have. He'd fall off the bull and I'd fix him up."

"So you've only had a professional relationship."

"Strictly professional." Aside from a few recent ridiculous fantasies she'd had about him.

"That's good," he said. "Mixing business with

pleasure can create a whole lot of problems. It usually doesn't turn out well for all parties involved."

According to Jenny, that didn't hold true in his case. "I assure you I will maintain absolute professionalism where Houston is concerned."

Dallas gave her a half smile. "I'm not worried about you at all. I don't necessarily trust Houston when it comes to being around an attractive woman."

"Believe me, Dallas, Houston isn't interested at all in me."

Four

Thanks to the sexy redhead back at the house, he was hotter than a firecracker in the desert on the fourth of July. Hotter than the grill he should be manning right now. But unless he pulled it together, he'd have to hide behind that grill all night to preserve his dignity.

Houston put away the pitchfork and considered taking a dip in the horse trough outside. Or getting the hell out of Dodge in his Dodge truck.

His gelding, Skip, raised his head from the hay bag in the stall long enough to nicker when Houston walked by. "I know, I know. Man up. But damn, she's one good-lookin' woman. Like you'd care about that. All you care about is eating, so get back to it and stop staring at me."

"Talkin' to horses now about your love life?"

Houston's gaze shot to the barn's entry to find his younger brother standing there, grinning like he'd won the lottery. "Shut up, Worth."

"Kiss my ass, Houston. Just because you've got it bad for a little gal you can't have doesn't mean you've got to take it out on me."

He brushed past Worth and strode down the drive leading to the house, ignoring Worth's laughter. Or trying to. But he couldn't ignore that his brother was quickly catching up with him. "Hold up, Houston. I think I know the answer to your dilemma."

He stopped and spun around on the heels of his frustration. "If you're going to suggest that I just go for it, I can't. She might very well be an employee here, and Dallas would skin me alive if I even looked like I might be interested in Jill outside of business. And there's the fact that she's barely given me the time of day since I met her two years ago."

"And that's the problem, Houston. You live for the chase and you can't stand it if she doesn't respond. That's why you need to act like you don't care one way or the other about her. That will take care of Dallas's worries and your girlfriend will soon be eating out of your good hand."

Of all the stupid assumptions. "She's not my girlfriend, dammit, and how do you know that's not what I've been doing?"

"Because I know you. You bring out the charm and toss out some innuendo and expect her to run to your bed. You're better off playing hard to get."

Houston started walking again. "You're mistaking me for someone else."

"Who?" Worth asked, meeting him stride for stride.

"You."

"Oh, hell, Houston. That's how we all operate. The apple doesn't fall far from the tree."

That just pissed him off. "I'm not a damn thing like our dad." Fed up with his brother's counsel, Houston quickened his pace and didn't look back, even when he reached the house. He tore open the door, walked through the deserted great room and into the kitchen to get another beer. When he heard the back door open, he glanced back from the refrigerator to see Worth leaving through it. Only then did he peer out the window to see Dallas flipping burgers and Austin crouched down nearby, talking to his son. Houston's mom and Jen were lounging by the pool, drinks in hand, while Jen talked non-stop. Fortunately, he could only see the back of Jill's head. *Unfortunately*, he discovered Worth had taken a seat beside her.

After releasing a rough breath, Houston popped the top on the can, took a long drink, geared up to face his current object of interest and vowed to intervene if his baby brother even leaned an inch her way.

Before he proceeded, he paused a moment to ponder Worth's words. Ignoring Jill would be the wisest course. Yeah, that's what he'd do—be polite but disinterested. No inappropriate comments. No suggestive looks. No damn fun whatsoever.

Armed with a plan, Houston pushed through the door and immediately homed in on Jill, seated, who was holding his nephew while Paris and Georgie looked on. When she caught sight of him, she smiled, showing off those damn cute dimples. All his good intentions threatened to blow away like the smoke coming from the barbecue.

He could do this. He could bypass the women and convene with the men. He could talk about rodeo or any kind of sport that didn't involve the bedroom, although that's exactly where his mind wandered. Luckily, his body didn't react. Yet.

He joined Dallas and held out his functioning hand. "Hand over the flipper. I'll take it from here."

Dallas shook his head. "I've got this now. If we'd waited for you, we'd all starve. What took you so long?"

Thoughts about the woman at the table behind him. "Just wanted to give you enough time to have a talk with Jill. How did it go?"

"Pretty good." Dallas lowered the grill's lid and turned toward him. "I think she'd be a great fit. She's a smart lady and seems to know her stuff. Greg Halbert told me she did."

"Who the hell is that?"

"Her boss."

"When did you call him?"

"Two weeks ago, before you dropped her name."

Now he was *really* confused. "I'm not following you, Dallas."

"I decided to check with the rodeo sports medicine programs to see if they could suggest any candidates for the job, like maybe an intern or two. Ben immediately mentioned Jill and said she was the only one he'd trust to run a program like ours. Then he threatened my jewels if I hired her away from him."

Great. "Does Jill know about this?"

"I'll let her know if she agrees to take the job."

"Do you think she will?" Damn, he sounded like an enthusiastic kid waiting to see if he'd gotten selected as a baseball all-star.

"I'm not sure, but I believe she could be leaning that way. She said she'd give me an answer by tomorrow before she heads back to Cowtown."

She wouldn't be heading back if Houston had his way. *Remember the "I don't care plan," Calloway.* "If she turns you down, we can always find someone else."

"Easier said than done," Dallas said. "Athletic trainers of her caliber and with her experience are snapped up pretty quick."

"Didn't realize that."

"Ben did mention some guy named Mike who's been in the business for twenty-five years. I could get in touch with him if this doesn't work out with Jill."

Houston didn't want some guy named Mike filling the position. Any guy for that matter. Truth was, he wanted Jill to go to work for them. He wanted *her*, plain and simple, right or wrong. Wise or not.

"Could you not say hello to your mother, *mijo*?"

Damn. Nobody got anything past Maria Calloway,

and no doubt she'd make a big deal over his injury. Might as well get it over with.

He turned around, muttered, "Sorry, Mom," then leaned over and kissed her cheek. "I just figured you and Jen were having one of your usual talks. I didn't want to interrupt."

"Jenny was doing all the talking." She lifted his hand to inspect his cast. "My son, you are a *torpe*."

"I'm not a klutz, Mom. Just unlucky sometimes."

"At least you'll be home for a while now, yes?"

"Yep." Unfortunately, and not because he didn't like being around family. He just didn't care for being off the circuit. "Did you meet Jill? Dallas might hire her to head up the medical team."

Her dark eyes narrowed as she flipped her gray-and-black braid over her shoulder. "I did meet her," she said, adding in a lowered tone, "*Ella es muy bonita*, so you best keep your lust to yourself."

Assumptions traveled fast on the ranch. "Just because I brought her here doesn't mean I'm lusting after her."

She patted his cheek. "*Mijo*, if the sun rises in the morning, you'll be lusting after a woman who looks like that."

Houston followed his mother's gaze to Jill, still sitting at the table, looking pretty as you please. And the only one who remained at that table with her happened to be his worthless brother. He said something to her, she laughed and Houston fumed.

He downed the rest of the beer and crumpled the can in his fist, itching to throw a punch. But that would be playing right into Worth's hand. It would also prove that what everyone else was thinking about him happened to be true—he had a belly full of lust for one beautiful athletic trainer.

Damn if he didn't, and he couldn't do a thing about it.

Houston didn't utter one word to Jill during dinner. In fact, he'd barely looked at her at all. Right now he seemed preoccupied with the conversation he was having with Worth by the pool. Clearly not a friendly conversation, in light of the body language. She knew all about sibling spats and wrote it off to a difference of opinion. Hopefully her ability to handle the workload wasn't up for debate during their discussion.

Jill turned her attention to Austin and Georgie's son sitting in a lawn chair, away from everyone else, looking a little forlorn. She might have assumed he could be bored, until she noticed the way he held his right arm. Her mind went back to Jenny talking about Chance's fall, and that only heightened her concern.

She raised her hand to get Georgie's attention and waved her over. "Got a quick question for you," she said when Georgie arrived at the table.

"Sure. What's up?"

"Jenny mentioned something about Chance falling off a fence this afternoon. Did you see how he landed?"

She could see a touch of panic growing in Georgie's eyes. "It happened so fast, and I was in the paddock treating a mare right before we were heading over here. When I ran over to Chance, he was kind of on one side. Why?"

"I've seen him favoring his arm a little."

Georgie whipped around to study her son. "I swear he never said a thing about anything hurting, and I asked him at least ten times. And you'd think since I'm a veterinarian, I would have noticed something."

"Don't worry," Jill said, bent on calming the nervous mother. "Children have been known to conceal their injuries from adults, especially little boys who want to be tough."

"That's my son, a chip off the old Austin block." Georgie attempted a smile before it rapidly disappeared. "Do you think it could be serious?"

"It could be nothing more than a bruise or a sprain. I could do a quick exam, if that's okay."

"I would so appreciate that," Georgie said in a grateful tone.

"Not a problem. It's what I do."

Georgie turned to her son and called, "Chance, come here for a minute."

The boy slid out of the seat and trudged over to his mom. "Are we going home now? I'm tired."

"In a minute," Georgie said. "Ms. Amherst wants to talk to you."

"Call me Jill, Chance," she said. "Does your arm hurt, sweetie?"

He shrugged only one of his shoulders, the first confirmation of her suspicions. "A little."

Jill swung the chair from beneath the table but remained seated. "Do mind if I take a look at it?"

He responded by shaking his head and moving in front of her. "I'm just going to touch your shoulder a little," she told him.

Chance looked more than a bit wary. "Is it going to hurt?"

Probably, but this was the only way she could diagnose the problem. "I'll be really gentle."

Jill ran two fingers along his clavicle and felt the deformity after very little exploration. When the boy winced, her suspicions turned to confirmation.

"That's all, Chance. You're a very brave young man." She looked up at Georgie. "He definitely has an injury to his collarbone."

Georgie's brown eyes went wide. "Oh, no. What do we do now?"

Jill stood and rested a palm on Chance's head. "Take him into an ER tonight for an X-ray to make sure I'm correct."

"And if it's fractured?"

"Most likely they'll put him in a splint until it heals." She didn't dare mention the dreaded S word—surgery—which could be a possibility.

Chance tugged on the hem of Georgie's T-shirt. "What's a splint, Mama?"

Jill jumped in when Georgie hesitated. "It's a wrap that goes around your shoulder to help it heal."

Chance suddenly looked somewhat excited. "Is it gonna look like that thing on Uncle Houston's hand?"

"Not exactly, but close. You'll have to wear it until

the doctor tells you it's okay." She glanced at Georgie. "Kids tend to heal faster than adults, so it could be as little as three weeks but usually six at the most. The doctor will probably instruct you to put some ice on it for a while."

Georgie gave Jill a quick hug. "You're an angel. Can I call you later if I have any questions once we get back from the ER?"

"Of course. Definitely let me know how he does."

"I will." Georgie regarded her son. "Tell Jill thank-you, honey."

"Thanks."

"You're welcome, sweetie. Get plenty of rest and you'll be back to climbing fences before you know it."

"Not if I can help it," Georgie muttered as she set out in the direction of her husband.

Soon after, Jill gave a final reassurance to the entire concerned family and said goodbye to them all as they cleared out, leaving her alone to remove the dinner remnants from the outdoor dining table since Houston had once again gone MIA.

She carried the plates and utensils into the almost clean kitchen—thanks to the mothers—and began loading the dishwasher, all the while wondering why Houston had brushed her off all evening for the most part. In fact, she only recalled him asking her to pass the mustard. Had it not been for his mother, stepmom and sisters-in-law, she might have spent the time alone in the corner, incessantly rolling the offer around in her mind. But she did appreciate the warm hospitality, the camaraderie, and found being around a good-hearted family quite refreshing. Dinner with her parents usually involved pretentious food and conversation centered on stocks, gossip and noncompliant children. She wondered if Houston recognized how lucky he'd been to be born into such a caring, down-to-earth group of people. She wondered if she'd even see him again to ask.

Jill suddenly sensed a presence behind her before she heard a deep, sensual voice asking, "What's a good-looking girl like you doing at a kitchen sink?"

Five

A dish tumbled out of Jill's hand and into the stainless-steel farm sink. She thanked her lucky stars she hadn't broken it when she nearly jumped out of her skin. "You startled me," she said as she placed the last plate in the washer. "I nearly shattered your china."

She sensed him moving closer, although little space separated them. "It's not exactly china, but you managed to rescue it, just like you rescued my nephew. That makes you an honest to goodness hero."

After drying her hands on a towel draped across the counter, Jill finally faced him, bringing them into even closer proximity. "I simply assessed the situation and made a recommendation. Nothing heroic about it."

Houston reached over and ran his fingertips down a strand of her hair, taking her by complete surprise for the second time in a matter of minutes. Had the seduction started?

"You had soap suds in your hair. Or maybe it was whipped cream from the pie."

So much for seduction. And why was that oddly disappointing? "I didn't have any pie, but I did rinse the dishes."

"Thanks for that, and since it looks like you're done, do you want to take a tour of the medical building?"

"I'd love to." She'd love to not feel so shaky around him. So aware of the scent of his cologne. The blanket of whiskers surrounding his mouth. The fact he was all alpha male and probably possessed plenty of talents in the bedroom…

"So are you ready to get after it?"

Her gaze snapped to his. "Excuse me?"

"The tour."

Good grief. *Get over it, Jillian.* "Lead the way."

She followed Houston out the front door and into the South Texas night. They walked the drive back to the main road serenaded by a chorus of cicadas. Only a slight breeze blew, providing little relief from the September heat.

Jill looked up at the sky highlighted by a host of stars and sighed. "The full moon is gorgeous tonight."

"Yeah, it is."

She glanced to her right and found him staring at her. "What's wrong?"

"Not a thing. You have a great profile."

"I have a nose that should be on a child."

"It's cute."

"It's my Irish heritage."

"But you have a darker complexion for a redhead."

She could almost hear what he was thinking—
if you're really a true redhead. "This is my natural
color, and I have some Spanish thrown into the gene
pool on my mother's side. That accounts for my skin
tone. How about you?"

"My mom is a fourth-generation Mexican Amer-
ican, and my dad's lineage is Old Norman French.
It sounds pretty sophisticated for a bunch of cow-
pokes, doesn't it?"

She couldn't help but smile. "It's always good to
know where you come from, but I'm surprised you,
Dallas and Austin don't look much alike."

"That's because we have the same father, but not
mother. Their mom died in a horse accident when
they were pretty young. My mom ended up being
their nanny, married our father and had me and Tyler
shortly after that."

Not quite as convoluted as she thought it might
be. "Okay. Then I assume your father divorced your
mother, married Jenny and had the twins."

Houston swiped a hand over his jaw. "Not exactly."

Perhaps she'd been mistaken about the convoluted
concept. "You don't have to explain if you don't want
to."

"The truth will come out sooner or later when you come to work for us."

If she came to work for them. "I'm all ears."

"My dad met up with Jen in New Orleans on a business trip. He ended up marrying her but he failed to divorce my mom. He spent most of his adulthood living a lie and working hard to cover it up."

Jill swallowed hard around her shock. "Then he was—"

"A bigamist. We found out at the reading of the will after he died. Learning you have twin half brothers and a stepmom was one helluva surprise straight out of a soap opera."

A colossal understatement. "You all seem to get along well, but I am a bit confused as to why Jenny would choose to live here, and why your mother would even allow it under the circumstances."

"Jenny came down a few summers ago to introduce us to Worth. They never left. And even though it seems like Jen and my mom don't get along, they're really pretty close. I'm sure they have a good time burning my dad in effigy for all his many sins."

She'd love to be a bug on the wall during some of those conversations. "I think it's great you all get along."

"All of us but Fort. He's still mad as hell at my dad and the brothers. We added Jen to the list after she decided to stay."

"Maybe he'll come around eventually."

"Not likely, but it's his loss. There's nothing more

important than family and friends. You don't know how much you appreciate them until they're gone."

Jill surmised that even in light of all his father's transgressions, Houston still missed him. She found that quite honorable—the willingness to forgive. If only she had the capacity where her own mother was concerned.

They walked the rest of the way in silence and arrived at the elaborate clinic a few minutes later. Jill stood by while Houston keyed a code into the pad. He opened the door and stepped to one side. "Here ya go. Your future place of employment."

She frowned at him. "You're jumping the gun a bit, aren't you?"

"We'll see after you take the tour."

Jill entered the building and moved into a large empty space with several windows and white tiled floors. Beyond that, she spotted several closed doors along the back wall. "This is a very blank canvas."

"And that's where you come in," Houston said. "Two of the rooms over there are for treatments. The other two are bathrooms, and in the corner a break room."

Evidently they'd thought of everything, except furnishings and equipment. "I'd like to see the treatment rooms."

"Sure. Follow me."

Their footsteps echoed in the expansive area as she trailed behind Houston. When they reached the closest room, he opened the door and once again, moved aside for her to inspect the premises.

She automatically went to the counter with the built-in sink and ran her hand over the stainless steel top. "Nice. Lots of room, too."

"And storage." As he reached around her to open the upper cabinet, his arm brushed against her arm and his injured wrist came to rest on her waist. Did he intend for that to happen, or was it simply an inadvertent gesture? Regardless, he didn't move his hand, and Jill remained glued to the spot, unsure what she should do next.

Speaking would be good. So would acting casual. Disinterested, as if a virile man's palm on her person was an everyday occurrence. "This will come in handy for all the supplies."

"You'll have free rein to order anything you think is necessary."

She thought it necessary that he give her some space before she did something stupid, like melt right into his fantastic arms. "That's good to know. Mind if I turn around now?"

"You don't need my permission to do that."

"I do need you to step back a little, otherwise I'm going to be rubbing, uh, bumping against your…" Manhood? Manliness? Oh, my. "Belt buckle."

"Rubbing and bumping. Sounds like one of those old-time disco dance moves, or a great time on a Saturday night."

Smooth, Jill. She couldn't believe she'd actually she used the word *rubbing*. Freud would have a field day with her. Houston was having a darn good time, too, if the amusement in his tone and the suggestion in his words was any indication.

Finally, he dropped his palm from her waist and moved back. She turned around to find him grinning like a well-practiced bad boy. "You're really having fun with my faux pas, aren't you?"

"Well, yeah. I'm used to hearing nothing but medical speak coming from that pretty mouth of yours. I have to admit I enjoy knowing you're not all business all the time."

"No, but only when it's appropriate and not in a professional setting."

"You're on my ranch."

"We're in a clinic. Granted, a clinic that's barely more than four walls and a couple of restrooms."

He sent her a mock frown. "Are you criticizing the accoutrements?"

"*Accoutrements?* Big word for a cowpoke."

"I know a few big words. I did graduate from college."

"Your major?"

"At first, female anatomy, but the extra homework took too much time away from the rodeo team so I changed it to business."

I will not laugh. I will not laugh. She laughed. "How long have you been using that line?"

He brushed her jawline with a fingertip. "First time. I'm just trying to keep you in a good mood."

She was in the mood all right, but not exactly for joking around. She'd always heard the term *palpable tension* but she hadn't experienced it…until now.

That realization, and the possibility of making a foolish mistake with an attractive-to-a-fault man, prompted her to make a more prudent suggestion. "We should head back to the house now. I need to take a shower."

He winked. "As a matter of fact, so do I."

Oh, boy. Oh, *man*. "I suppose you're going to say if we shower together, we could conserve water."

He moved beside her and leaned a hip against the cabinet, one elbow resting on the counter. "Nope, I wasn't, but if that would make you feel more welcome in my home, I'm game."

Oh, boy, did that unearth some unbelievable mental pictures. "I'm feeling quite welcome as it is, and I'm sure you make enough money to pay the water bill."

"Leave it to you to go from fantasies to finances."

She playfully slapped at his arm. "Okay. Stop trying to flirt with me."

"Hey, you were the one who wanted to take a joint shower." He winked. "That's still on the table if you change your mind."

She pointed at the open door. "Let's go. Now. Before I…"

"Before you what?"

Before she kissed him like some smitten buckle bunny. "Before I fall asleep on my feet. I'm still trying to recover from Jenny's drink."

He pushed away from the counter. "You didn't even finish the drink, but then you are a lightweight, Amherst."

"And you can be a pain in the butt, Calloway."

"It's part of my charm. Too bad you don't appreciate it."

There, Jill thought. Back to their usual insulting banter. The world was now tilted correctly on its axis. All was good and right.

Still, something had changed between them. Subtle, but still apparent. A sensual connection, she feared. Now that she acknowledged exactly how this might go if she wasn't incredibly careful, Jill pledged to keep their liaison platonic and their relationship somewhat contentious, as it had been in the past.

But after spending practically the past twenty-four hours with Houston Calloway, and liking it, only time would tell if she could rewind that clock.

If he could turn back time, Houston would do it, just so he could watch Jill walk back into the room. She wore a loose, light blue T-shirt stamped with "Quick Responder" and white shorts that gave him an eyeful of her long, long legs. She still had on a bra but she didn't have on shoes and he was kind of surprised to see pink painted toenails. Hell, even her feet were sexy. Her hair looked sexy, too, pulled up into a high ponytail and obviously still damp. If he'd coaxed that shower out of her, he would've made sure she was downright wet.

Stop lusting, mijo...

What a fine time for his mother to jump into his head. Probably not a bad thing. He'd already blown Worth's advice about ignoring her right out of the water like a duck decoy. Time to regroup. Time to put the plan back into action.

When Jill walked right up to the sofa and studied him head to toe, the plan began to slither away again. "It's so weird to see you dressed in shorts and a T-shirt, Calloway."

"I could say the same about you, Amherst." Although he wouldn't call it weird. He'd call it damn good.

"Is that your bedtime attire?" she asked.

For him naked was bedtime attire, a fact he would keep to himself for the moment. "Nah. I usually wear my chaps, but I sent them out for a good cleaning."

"That would be really weird." She smiled, sat at the opposite end of the couch and curled her legs beneath her. "Have you thought about being a cowboy stand-up comic when you retire from the rodeo?"

"Nope, because I don't plan to retire anytime soon."

She tightened the ponytail and adjusted the throw pillow at her back. "How long have you been competing?"

He had to stop and think about that. "I guess I rode my first bull when I was fifteen, so that would be almost sixteen years."

"So you're thirty going on thirty-one."

"How old did you say you were?" he asked.

She tried to look insulted but failed. She just looked damn beautiful. "Didn't your mother teach you it's impolite to ask a lady her age?"

"Yeah, but first of all, I recall you said you're a

year younger than Worth. Second, I've never understood why that's such a big deal."

"Me, either. And to refresh your memory, I'm twenty-six."

"Dallas mentioned you used to ride horses."

She brought her knees up and hugged them to her chest, giving him a glimpse of the back of her thighs. "I did ride. A long time ago."

"What made you stop?"

When she shifted slightly, Houston figured he'd hit a nerve. "It's sort of a sad story."

Sad he didn't need, but he sensed she need to talk. He did have to be careful not to push her. He wouldn't want anyone to pressure him when it came to his secrets, and he still had one he'd never told a living soul. Not even his own mother. "I've got all night to hear the story, but only if you want to tell it."

"Actually, it's not all bad," she said. "That long-ago event drove me to help others."

He wondered if it involved her having some sort of bad accident. That would sure explain why she was so protective and persistent when it came to her patients. "How did that come about?"

She hesitated a split second before speaking again. "I guess it all started when I was around five and I learned to ride. Two years later, I wanted something more challenging than going around an arena, so I learned how to jump. I remember how exhilarating it was that first time."

"I remember feeling the same way when I stayed on

a bull for eight seconds." And the first time he'd had sex. Something he didn't need to consider right then.

"Well, I guess we have that in common," she said with an uneasy smile.

They had more in common than he cared to admit. "I guess so."

"When I was about fifteen," she continued, "I was heavy into competition, and so was my boarding school roommate and best friend, Millie. We used to spend weekends going to events together, and we practiced almost every day together at the school's stables. She was such an incredible person. So full of life and much more daring than I ever was."

"She took higher jumps?"

"No. She used to sneak out the window and meet up with boys from the nearby military academy."

"Did you ever go with her?"

"Not hardly. My mother drilled me my entire formative years about the dangers of teenage sex. 'You'll get a disease, Jillian' or 'You'll get pregnant, Jillian.'"

"No 'You'll go blind, Jillian'?"

"Luckily, she never said that, the only thing that saved me from total sexual frustration."

After she blushed and looked away, Houston inched closer and touched her shoulder to reassure her. "Hey. Don't be embarrassed, Jill. When nature calls, you best answer or you *will* go blind."

She tried to smile but it fell flat. "Funny, Millie used to talk about that. The nature thing, not the going blind thing." She paused and sighed. "When I lost her, I felt like a part of me went with her."

Houston could only speculate why the relationship ended. "Did you two have a fight?"

"She died."

That he hadn't expected. He also couldn't help but notice the lack of emotion in her tone, but the pain in her green eyes spoke volumes. He could be entering dangerous waters, but he had to ask. "What happened to her?"

"We were competing one Saturday during the summer when we were home on break. Her horse balked at the jump and she was thrown." She paused to take a breath. "But in usual Millie fashion, she stood up, brushed herself off and got back on her mare to finish the course. Everyone thought she was okay. I thought she was okay. But it turned out that wasn't the case at all."

The first sign of tears began to appear in her eyes, leading Houston to grab a tissue holder from the coffee table and offer it to her. "You don't have to keep going, Jill.'"

She laid the box in her lap and lifted her chin slightly. "I'm okay. I need to tell you everything, although I'm not sure why." She drew in another deep breath and let it out slowly. "I talked to her on the phone that night. We were supposed to sleep over at my house but she complained about having a headache. She told me she was going to take a pain reliever and go to bed early. The next morning, the maid couldn't get her to wake up. They rushed her to the hospital, but it was too late. She'd had a brain bleed. She passed away that afternoon."

He reached over and took her hand. "I'm sorry, sweetheart. That had to be tough."

"It was. Very tough. I realized later that if someone with medical knowledge had been present, they would have known what to look for. They would have assessed her to see if she had a concussion. At the very least, they would have kept her from getting back on the horse. Although we have no way of knowing for certain, continuing to ride and jump could have caused a secondary impact, which could have led to the bleed. Someone should have been there to tell her not to take certain pain medication."

He'd had a lot of experience with the "could haves" and "should haves," so he understood exactly where she was coming from. He also understood why she was so protective of her patients, and he felt kind of bad how he'd treated her in the past. "Second-guessing can be a bitch, can't it?"

"Definitely. I still do it from time to time, but the experience has made me a very diligent athletic trainer. I take nothing for granted when it comes to taking care of athletes."

Houston realized that with every cowboy or cowgirl she'd treated, and possibly saved, she'd had her best friend in mind. "One thing's for sure. Loss changes people, sometimes for the better." But not necessarily in his case.

"I was never quite the same in so many ways, but I still have great memories." She snapped a tissue from the holder and dabbed at her eyes. "We called ourselves soul twins, Millie and Jilly. We both had rich parents and one obnoxious sibling, only she had a younger brother. He's still a spoiled jerk."

Now he knew why she didn't like him calling her Jilly. That had been reserved for a longtime friend. "So you stayed in touch with her family?"

"Not by choice," she said in an angry tone. "Jilly's brother is marrying my sister next weekend."

His life might be a soap opera, but hers sounded like a well-heeled incestuous mess. "Tough break."

"They deserve each other. Millie deserved to live. Not a day goes by when I don't think about her. When I don't wish I had told her how much she meant to me."

Houston could seriously relate to that. When he thought back to what he'd said and done the day before his father died, it made him sick. It also disturbed him to see her hurting that badly, so he did what instinct dictated—he scooted to her side and put his arm around her.

He wouldn't have been surprised if she pulled away. Rejected the gesture. Instead, she rested her head on his shoulder. They stayed that way for quite a while, until she finally raised her head. The look she gave him was all too familiar, and he'd bet his last buck he knew what she wanted. Trouble was, he worried about the repercussions of answering her request. But when she cupped his jaw with her palm, and pulled his mouth to hers, only a fire on the living room floor could have stopped him.

He brought her into his lap, all the while thinking this wasn't a good idea. She was vulnerable and her motivation for doing this had a lot to do with her emotional state. But when she snuggled up against him, all bets were off.

Houston tried to keep the kiss light, keep it controlled. Keep it restrained. Jill had other ideas. She met his tongue stroke for stroke, wriggled in his lap and he'd begun to believe she had no intention of putting an end to the torment until he gave her what she wanted. What he wanted. But at what cost?

He reacted as any man would, with a strong stirring beneath his shorts and the need to touch her. As he ran his palm up her thigh, he felt her shiver, and he knew he had to find the strength and some way to stop before he couldn't.

His pocket began to vibrate, followed by a classic country honky-tonk song. He could ignore it, or view it as a good excuse to halt this craziness before they reached that point of no return. Answering the call would be the better part of valor. Saved by the bell or, in this case, a ringtone.

With that in mind, he gently slid her off his lap and groaned, then fished the phone out of his pocket.

Austin. Normally he'd curse his brother's bad timing, but not tonight.

He cleared his throat before he answered. "Hey, Austin."

"Hey, Houston. What's up?"

Bad choice of words. "Not much. What's going on with you?"

"Georgie told me to report to Jill after we took Chance to the ER."

Houston felt like jerk for not remembering his nephew's injury. He glanced at Jill to see she had her hand pressed against her lips, looking slightly shell shocked. He wasn't sure she was in any shape to take the call. "She's busy right now. Tell me what the doctor said and I'll relay it to her."

"Chance has a fractured collarbone, just like she said. He has a splint, also like she said, and he's going to be back to normal in a few weeks. Tell Jill we owe her one."

Houston owed her an apology for letting things get out of hand. "I'll let her know, and I'm glad he's going to be okay."

"So are we. And, Houston, just a few words of advice."

Great. More brotherly advice. "About what?"

"We all really like Jill, and we'd like to have her as part of the team. Try not to screw it up by making a move on her."

It could be too late for that. "Message received. Tell the kid to hang in there and I'll see him tomorrow. We can compare injuries."

"Will do."

After hanging up, Houston set the phone on the table and regarded Jill again, who thankfully looked a bit more composed. "That was Austin. He said your diagnosis was correct and they wanted to thank you for helping out."

She clutched a pillow to her chest. "I'm just glad he's going to be okay."

"Are you okay?"

"That's still up in the air after what I just did."

"You weren't alone. I could have put a stop to it."

"Why didn't you?"

"Honestly? I didn't want to. But just so you know, I wasn't going to let it go any further."

"We shouldn't have gone there at all, but it really was my fault. I don't know what came over me."

"You were running on emotion. You were just looking for comfort."

"But that's not like me at all."

"It was only a kiss, Jill. No big deal."

"Well, that makes me feel better. I realize it's been a while since I've kissed anyone, but I didn't think it was that bad."

Not in the least. In fact, it was real good. "Do you hear me complaining?"

She finally smiled. "No, but I really hoped you would break out into song. I thought you had until I realized it was your phone."

"If I was going to sing to you, it wouldn't be a song about my tractor."

They both laughed then, and that helped ease the burden Houston was carrying around because he hadn't shown a scrap of restraint. But all humor disappeared when Jill's expression turned serious again.

"This could really complicate everything," she

said. "I can't accept the position if I know this is going to be a problem."

He wasn't ready to throw in that towel just yet. "It won't be a problem at all as long as we maintain the boundaries."

"No more kisses."

"That's probably best." But now that he'd sampled her skills, it wouldn't be easy.

"We operate on a strictly professional level from this point forward."

Unacceptable as far as he was concerned. "You wouldn't be working for me, so I don't see any reason why we can't be friends."

She pointed at him. "Friends with no benefits."

Damn. "If that's what it takes for you to come on board, then that's what we'll be." Now for the all-important question. "Does this mean you're going to take the job?"

She pushed off the sofa and stood. "It means I'm going to bed. I'll let you know my answer in the morning."

He came to his feet. "You're going to keep me in suspense until then?"

She strolled across the room and paused at the opening leading to the hall. "You're a tough guy. You can handle waiting a little longer."

With that, Jill disappeared, leaving Houston to question their agreement. He didn't care much for science, but he could recognize chemistry between two people. Could he be only her friend without wanting more? But in reality, that would only be until he hit the road again to return to the rodeo. Still, spending a couple of months with a woman he wanted, and couldn't have, would be torture. Then again, she could turn down the job. Problem solved.

He'd worry about that tomorrow. Tonight, he planned to go to bed and let the fantasies about Jill Amherst fly.

Six

Jill hadn't slept more than four hours last night. Instead, she'd relived the kiss a hundred times, and tried to disregard how Houston had made her feel. But she couldn't ignore the guilt over laying her feelings bare, and making the first inadvisable move. She could chalk her conduct up to emotional upheaval, or the very real fact her attraction to him had grown due to his kindness. And this morning she would have to confront the reason for her restlessness. Putting it off would only delay the inevitable.

On that thought, Jill climbed out of the bed and went through her normal routine, twisted her hair into a low ponytail, then dressed in khakis, casual flats and a blouse. Once in the great room, she followed the scent of coffee into the kitchen and came across Houston seated at the center island, dressed in a light chambray shirt and denim jeans. He didn't bother to look up from the laptop before him when she entered the room.

"Mind if I have a cup?" she asked on the way to the coffeemaker.

He still hadn't even ventured a glance at her. "Help yourself. Mugs are in the cabinet next to the sink. Cream's in the fridge and sugar's in a canister next to the coffeepot."

Jill located the cups and ignored the white one that said Bull Riders Stay on Longer. After pouring the brew into an innocuous blue mug, she joined Houston at the island and slid onto the stool opposite him.

Since he still refused to look at her, she decided to start the conversation with small talk. "Catching up on current events?"

"Catching up on circuit standings and checking out a new ad campaign."

"Ad campaign?"

"Yeah. I did some advertisements for a company that makes compression wraps."

"What kind of advertisements?"

"Internet and a few TV spots but mostly billboards."

His face splashed across an oversize roadside sign could distract more than a few female drivers. "Is it a national campaign?"

"Yep."

His apparent inability to even venture a glance at her was somewhat frustrating. "I just wanted to say how much I appreciated your friendship last night. You really are a good listener." And a phenomenal kisser, which she would not mention.

He closed the laptop's lid and finally met her gaze. "No problem, but I'm still pretty mad at myself this morning."

Here we go. "You didn't do anything but listen to my story."

"But I wasn't acting too gentlemanly. You were hurting and I should have realized that. I feel like I took advantage."

She'd *wanted* him to take advantage. "I kissed you, remember, not the other way around."

"Yeah, but I sure as hell didn't protest. If Austin hadn't called, it might have gone further, and we both might have regretted it."

True, it would have been a huge misstep. Perhaps a pleasurable one, but a mistake all the same. "Lacking a little in the willpower department, are we?"

He cracked a crooked smile. "It's your fault for being so damn sexy."

Sexy? "You're forgiven."

He slid off the stool and stood. "Finish your coffee and let's go."

"Where?"

"I have a few more places to show you around the ranch."

"You haven't even asked if I've reached a decision."

"I feel like you're still on the fence, so I'm hoping what you see this morning will push you over to our side."

He'd nailed it. She had yet to make up her mind. Making out with Houston should have convinced her to walk away. Or run. Yet she couldn't allow a moment of weakness to ruin what could be the opportunity of a lifetime.

After taking another drink of the coffee, Jill came to her feet. "Just let me change into my sneakers and we can go."

"No need," he said. "We're not going walk."

"Are we traveling by truck or horseback?"

"Neither. We'll take one of the ATVs because it's already hot as hell outside."

The joys of South Texas weather in late summer. Fortunately when they climbed onto the two-seater and took off, it generated enough breeze to offer Jill some relief. Yet by the time they stopped in front of the mountain-sized lodge behind a van, she felt as if she'd been in a sauna, dressed in a parka.

"They're still doing some finishing touches on the lodge," Houston said after the climbed out of the vehicle. "I swear the damn thing will never be finished."

Jill highly doubted the Taj Mahal was built in a day. "It's a big place."

"Yeah, it is. I'd take you inside but I don't want to get in the workers' way and force any more delays."

That disappointed her. "I understand."

"That's not what I want to show you anyway. Follow me."

She did, past the lodge's front facade and around the corner. He opened a gate to a courtyard with a pool in the center of what appeared to be a series of apartments. "What is this?"

"Where you'll be living when you come to work for us."

She decided not to correct him on the "when" thing and opted to enjoy the tour. They crossed over the deck and Houston paused at the first unit, pounded a code into a keypad and opened the door.

Jill stepped into an amazing living space open to an equally stellar kitchen, complete with gorgeous black slate appliances, gray cabinets and marble countertops. Beyond that, a sliding glass door revealed a private, fenced-in patio.

The whole place was awe-inspiring given they were employee quarters. She'd expected something less elaborate and more along the lines of a bunkhouse. "This is extremely nice."

"It's only one bedroom," Houston said. "But it's a nice bedroom."

He pointed out a half bath in the small hall, then led her to the sleeping quarters that looked a hundred times better than the motels Jill had occupied in the past two years. Attached to that, a spacious bathroom with a huge soaking tub and a stand-alone shower, all decked out in marble opulence.

"Jen decorated this one and one other," Houston said. "The rest are more in line for male support staff."

She imagined barn wood and leather. "It's great, but I don't have any furniture."

"Not a problem. You can pick out what you want."

This all seemed much too good to be true. "I admit this is fairly tempting."

"Good. I have one more thing to persuade you."

"I can't imagine what that would be."

He started across the room. "Believe me, you'll be impressed."

She noticed the impressive fit of his jeans, his confident gait and the width of his back as she walked behind him. The fact she noticed all those attributes nudged her back into relying on her head, not her desires. She had to weigh the problems that could arise should they cross a line they had no business crossing. Still, they had established the friendship boundary last night, and it seemed Houston was determined to abide by the terms.

After they returned to their transportation, Houston drove back up the road and stopped at an expansive metal barn adjacent to the lodge. She trailed behind him down the stable's alley, where he paused at one stall.

"I'd like you to meet Gabby," Houston said. "She's a good old girl."

Jill inched her way to his side to see a bay mare sticking her muzzle between the railings. "She's beautiful."

"She's the only Thoroughbred on the place. Tyler traded for her when a couple nearby wanted a quarter horse gelding for their son so he could learn to rope. She's supposed to be a great English horse."

"And I doubt any of the Calloway boys ride English."

"Not a chance." He turned and smiled for the first time today. "But you do, and I figure you could take her out for a ride now and then."

Jill put up her hands, palms forward. "Wait a minute. I haven't ridden in over a decade." Not since the accident.

"Then it's way past time you get back on and remember how great it feels to ride."

She lowered her eyes to study the pavement beneath her feet. "I don't know if I want to remember."

Houston touched her face, causing her to look up. "I wouldn't force anything on you, but maybe you should start moving forward, not backward. Take a few chances. Get busy living. And I'll be here if you need a little push in that direction now and then."

A solid truth rang out in his words, and Jill realized she had been holding back in so many ways. She'd subconsciously crawled into a social cell, burying herself in her career to keep from feeling. The same routine day in and day out, holding everyone in her life at arm's length. Change wouldn't come easy, but the time had come to try.

"I guess I could get back on a horse again, but first things first. I have a lot of work to do around here."

His expression brightened. "Does that mean—"

"Yes. I'm ready to join the Texas Extreme team."

Houston grabbed Jill off her feet and swung her

around and she felt petite for the first time in her life. She also felt winded and wild and even a little nervous, particularly as he lowered her down his body, slowly. When he kept his gaze trained on hers, she experienced a spark along with a touch of heat. He didn't immediately let her go. She didn't automatically wrest herself out of his arms. They simply stood there a few moments, until the horse nickered, as if she'd nominated herself as their equine chaperone.

Jill came to her senses and stepped back. "Don't do that again, Calloway. I can't do my job if you break my ribs."

"At least you could heal yourself."

"Very amusing." She wrapped her arms around her middle. "So what's next?"

He sent her a sly smile. "What do you want to do?"

She thought of several answers, none that would be suitable, or wise. "I suppose I need to break the news to my boss. Fortunately I'm not on the schedule for three weeks, so he should have time to find a replacement."

"Guess I should go tell Dallas the news, unless you want to do it."

"You have my permission. Besides, if it weren't for you, I wouldn't be here."

His expression went suddenly solemn. "I'm glad you're here, Jill. We're all glad you're here. Welcome to the Calloway family."

That took her aback. "I wouldn't go that far, Houston. I'm just an employee."

He smiled again. "Believe me, they'll see it differently. In fact, I won't be a bit surprised if they throw you a party."

As it turned out, Houston had been right. He escorted Jill to the main house later that evening, where they were met with a round of applause and a spread of food laid out on tables on the front porch.

Jen stepped forward first, as usual. "We're so glad you're with us, Jill!"

Houston stood back while one by one, the women hugged Jill, except for his mother, who only briefly patted her on the back. Maria's behavior didn't shock him. She'd always been cautious when it came to women, especially if she thought they had staked a claim on one of the sons for all the wrong reasons. Particularly him. She'd be proud to know he'd barely touched Jill since that mind-blowing kiss. Except for that unplanned grab-and-go earlier in the barn when he'd wanted to kiss her again. And not being able to do it was killing him.

Dallas came out onto the porch next, followed by Austin, Worth and, bringing up the rear, Tyler. He had a bone to pick with that brother over his abandonment in Cowtown, but he'd wait until later. Or not, he thought, when Tyler walked over to Jill and pulled her into a bear hug.

Houston instantly moved forward like he was protecting his territory. But Jill wasn't anyone's property, and she sure as hell didn't need protecting.

Try telling Tyler that, Houston thought when his

brother draped his arm around Jill's shoulder. "This woman is the angel of the rodeo," he said. "She rescued me more times than I can count."

Jill glanced at Houston before returning her attention back to Tyler. "How is your knee, by the way?"

"It's great, thanks to you. PT saved my season last year. You saved my season."

Disgusted by the scene, Houston turned his back, grabbed a plate from the table and began filling it with taquitos and chips and some sort of round thing with spinach. Normally he'd complain that this wasn't enough stuff to feed a squirrel, but he'd pretty much lost his appetite. Besides, he needed to occupy his good hand in order not to punch Tyler.

What the hell was wrong with him? Jill was free to do as she pleased with whoever she pleased. He had no call to be jealous or mad or even concerned. But he was. He still wanted to be her friend, and he also wanted benefits. A lot of benefits…

"Do you want to go over your benefits while you're here, Jill?" Dallas asked from behind him.

"We can cover that later," she answered.

Houston wanted to cover her in a few ways she wouldn't forget. With his working hand. With his mouth. Talk about some mighty fine benefits. But she might prefer to be tied up with Tyler, and that thought made him angry all over again, although that made no sense whatsoever. He'd never viewed his younger brother as competition, but then they'd never competed over a woman before.

He turned to find Jill occupied with another guy,

only this one didn't wear a cowboy hat and ride bucking bronc. This one had a pacifier in his mouth and a fistful of her hair. She looked like a natural mother with a baby in her arms, all the more reason for him to steer clear. Had a lot of rodeo left in him before he traveled down domestic drive. She might want a man who'd give her lots of babies before that old biological clock began to drive her crazy. He wasn't ready for the responsibility of changing diapers and planning for a kid's college fund.

Jill claimed a spot on the glider next to Paris. "Does he sleep all night?" she asked.

Paris took a squirming Luke from Jill and smoothed a hand over his head. "Most of the time."

"And when he doesn't," Austin began, "I get up and walk him around until I'm sleepwalking."

All the confirmation Houston needed to avoid the parent trap. He couldn't very well tend to an infant when he still ran the circuit. And he wouldn't quit the circuit until he was good and ready, in about ten years.

He took a seat in a rocker and picked at his food while the rest of the crowd filled their plates. Once everyone settled into their seats, Jen announced, "I believe I'll make some juleps for this celebration." When she was met with a chorus of simultaneous noes she looked highly insulted. "You people are no fun," she said. "I suppose I'll just have to make my famous lemonade."

"Good idea," Maria said. "And don't go sneaking in some vodka."

While the conversation continued, Houston hung back to watch for any sign Jill was tiring of all the questions. Then his mom pulled her chair closer to the glider and he immediately sensed trouble.

"You said you're from Florida. What city?"

"Ocala. It's about eighty miles north of Orlando."

"What do your parents do?"

"My father is an investment banker. My mother is a social butterfly."

Maria leaned back. "So you're rich."

Houston couldn't stay silent any longer. "That's enough, Mom. She's not on trial here."

"It's okay," Jill said. "Yes, my parents have money. So did their parents and their parents' parents."

"Are you an only child, sugar?" Jenny chimed in.

"Actually, no. I have a younger sister, Pamela, and that reminds me…" She looked directly at Dallas. "I forgot to mention that Pamela's wedding is next weekend. I'm supposed to attend, but if you'd prefer I stay here, I'd understand."

"We wouldn't hear of it," Jenny said before Dallas could open his mouth. "It would be blasphemous for a woman not to attend her sister's wedding. She wouldn't have nearly enough time to replace a bridesmaid."

Jill looked away for a minute. "I'm not in the wedding party. She's left that to ten of her closest friends."

"That's terrible," Georgie said. "I don't have any siblings but if I did, they sure would have been in my wedding."

Jill smiled. "Believe me, it's not a problem. We've never been close, or haven't been in a long time."

"Regardless," Jen began, "I'm sure your mother would be disappointed if you didn't show up."

He could see a hint of anger in Jill's eyes. "My mother would be disappointed if I didn't show up to meet a whole slew of husband candidates from the local country club. I would miss seeing my father. However, if you absolutely would prefer I stay, Dallas, you'd be doing me a favor."

"I have a better idea," Paris said. "What if you take one of the brothers along with you as a pretend boyfriend? That way you could see your father and get your mother off your back."

Jen clapped her hands together. "That's a wonderful idea, Paris. We have three available, all very handsome and single."

Worth stepped forward. "I can rearrange my schedule and go."

Tyler punched him on the upper arm. "No way. You'd get run off before the end of the reception for flirting with all the female guests. I'll go."

The more the banter between the brothers continued, the madder Houston got. Truth was, he didn't trust either Worth or Tyler any further than he could hurl them.

And when Jill sent him a *save-me* look, he figured it was time he stepped in.

"Neither of you will go," Houston said, drawing everyone's attention.

"I agree," Dallas added. "We can't count on the

two of you not to make a move on her before the plane took off."

"I still think it's a wonderful idea," Jenny said. "And I also think it's best that Jill choose which brother to take."

"I'm the logical choice," Tyler added. "But Jen's right. It should be her choice."

Worth inched toward Jill and winked. "Sometimes it's not about logic."

"You're all crazy," Maria said. "You haven't even asked the *chica* if she wants an escort."

All eyes turned to Jill, who just sat there, mouth agape.

Not a problem. He'd go ahead and speak for her. "If anyone is going to take her to Florida, it's going to be me."

"Have you lost your mind, Houston?"

"No, and would you slow down, dammit?"

Jill quickened the pace as she strode across his driveway. If she had her way, she'd beat him into the house and hide away in the guest room until he gave up.

But he was too fast for her, she realized when she reached the porch and he clasped her arm, bringing her to a stop and turning her around before she had a chance to open the door.

She'd been only a few feet from escape. "Look, I'm tired. Can't we just discuss this in the morning?"

"Give me ten minutes to argue my case."

"Five minutes."

"Fine."

She moved into the great room and glanced at the couch where they'd had the monumental talk the night before. Where she'd crazily kissed him. She opted to keep going through the kitchen and onto the patio to avoid a repeat performance, as if the sofa held some sort of magical powers of persuasion. That would be the cowboy behind her.

Once outside, Jill chose a deck chair by the pool while Houston selected the one beside her. She stared at the backlit blue water and under normal circumstances, she might take a dip. But she found nothing normal about taking a pretend boyfriend home to meet the folks.

She shifted toward Houston and said, "Your five minutes start now."

He leaned back and crossed his long, jeans-covered legs at the ankles. "First of all, although I didn't come up with this plan, Jen has a good idea. If you don't want the hassle of your mother trying to set you up with some guy, it makes sense for you to bring your own. Second, both my younger brothers would be draped all over you like a cheap shirt."

"And you wouldn't," she said in a simple statement of fact, and hopefully without any disappointment in her tone.

"Not unless we agreed to mutual draping."

Oh, that grin and those deadly eyes. "Interesting concept. The BYOB, bring your own boyfriend, not the draping. But this isn't a sorority mixer, Houston. This is a wedding."

"You have a point, but have you thought about doing it just for fun?"

She'd never been one to do anything only for fun, and that had kept her out of trouble. "I can't imagine pretending you and I are a couple being all that much fun, especially if we slip up."

"We'd have to make sure that didn't happen."

"How do you propose we do that?"

He rubbed his stubbled jaw. "Well, we'd have to act like we like each other."

"Which would involve a certain amount of affection, I assume."

"We could hold hands. I could kiss your cheek now and then."

"Are you going to chase me on the playground, too?"

He smiled. "Sure, as long as you let me catch you now and then."

"Maybe." Had she really sounded that coy?

A span of silence passed before Houston spoke again. "Here's something else to consider. You said your mother wouldn't approve if you brought a cowboy home."

"Or a professional poker player."

"I could say I play poker when I'm not competing."

"Double whammy. I like that."

"There you go. You'd be sending the message to your mom that you're going to make your own decisions when it comes to who you choose to date, and maybe she'll stop trying to fix you up."

"Or I could just tell her to stop fixing me up."

He looked confused. "Haven't you told her that before?"

"Truthfully, yes."

"How's that working for you?"

"Not well."

"Point made."

Yes, he had made a few valid points, and seeing her mother's reaction to having a cowboy in the house would be priceless. However, that would only be a temporary fix to her mother's matchmaking efforts. Still, it could be worth it...

Jill had one important question to ask her possible escort. "What's in it for you, Houston?"

He shifted in the seat. "Just helping out a friend. Besides, I don't have anything better to do this weekend. And who would want to turn down a trip to Florida?"

Any man who'd ever met her mother. "You *do* realize I'm being forced to make two major decisions in one day."

"One down, one to go."

"This one might be tougher than the last."

He pushed out of the chair and pulled her up, right into his arms. "Let's practice."

"Practice what?"

"We need to see if we can do this pretend thing. If you cringe every time I touch you, it won't work."

She'd never cringed around him. Exactly the opposite. "I can handle it, Houston."

He nudged her closer, pressed his palms on the

small of her back and lowered his voice. "We're on a dance floor with your family looking on. I tell you they're watching. What do you do now?"

"Tell them to stop ogling us?"

He tipped her cheek against his shoulder. "You relax. You pretend you like being in my arms."

She wouldn't be pretending. "Okay."

He tucked her hair behind one ear and kissed her cheek lightly. "You look up at me and smile. I lean over and whisper—" he brought his lips to her ear, causing her to shiver "—'I could use a beer.'"

With the spell now broken, she batted her eyelashes and spoke through a fake smile. "Do I look like your servant?"

"I didn't know you were into role playing."

She should probably yank out of his arms, but she felt like someone had cemented her to his chest. "Only if you're *my* servant."

"I'm game if you are."

The tension between them created a clear and present danger. Jill wanted to tell him to shut up and kiss her, but she didn't have to. He brushed his lips across hers, once, twice before he swooped in. He kept it gentle, kept it soft, kept her wanting more with each sensual stroke of his tongue. He slid his hands down to her bottom and pressed against her, sending the unmistakable message that this little mouth action had raised the sail. She could relate. The heat and dampness she experienced was almost foreign to her, and she knew if this interlude didn't end, they could be tossing away the no-benefits clause.

As if Houston sensed the same thing, he broke all contact, cleared his throat and stepped back. "You passed the test. I'm convinced."

Jill was only convinced of one thing—she hadn't wanted it to end. "You do realize if I agree to this, we can't have a lot of that happening."

"But we can have some of it?"

"Yes…no…" Heavens, her mind had been blown to bits. "We have to be sensible. After we return to the ranch, it's back to business as usual." Which sounded like anything would go in Florida. "We'll discuss this further in the morning."

"Sounds like a plan."

When Houston crossed his arms and pulled off his shirt, Jill was momentarily rendered speechless. "What are you doing?"

"I'm going to take a swim. Wanna join me?"

Oh, wow, did she ever. But she wouldn't. "I'm heading for the shower," she said as she began to back away.

"Suit yourself, but you have a giant bathtub at your disposal right here."

She also had a man with a monumental set of muscles and an amazing chest standing before her. "I'll pass, but you go ahead and enjoy your *bath*."

The minute Houston began to undo his buckle, Jill spun around and hurried into the house. But extreme curiosity or feminine insanity sent her to the small window to peer out into the yard. She caught a glimpse of Houston's bare butt before he dove into the pool, and it was more than enough to spark her imagination.

She had absolutely no idea what had gotten into her. Well, actually, yes she did. Houston Calloway had crawled right under her skin. And now she had to decide if she would allow him to accompany her home.

She could choose the path of least resistance and go alone, or she could take a chance and let whatever happened happen. She could be cautious, or she could be carefree.

Deep down she recognized she would have to be strong if she accepted Houston's offer, and she wasn't certain she possessed that much strength. For that reason, she leaned toward nixing the whole plan and going the safe route.

That would probably be best for all concerned. The wisest course, and she'd always given a lot of credence to wisdom. She saw no reason to veer from that now.

Yes, she did. Perhaps the time had come to pull out all the stops. To finally learn what she'd been missing. To take a risk with a man she could trust. Yet she had no way of knowing if Houston was that man.

In order to find out, she could learn through personal experience, or she could search for a few personal references. And she knew just where to go for those.

"That was so much fun!"

Jill slid onto the bar stool across from Paris and

set two bags on the ground beneath the small round table. "It was tons of fun, but I feel bad that you had to be gone from the baby so long."

Paris shrugged. "Dallas could use some dad time with him, and now that he's eating solid foods, Luke isn't that dependent on me. Besides, it's time someone else did some diaper duty."

They shared in a few laughs before Jill set out on her information gathering. "Dallas seems like a natural father, and so does Austin. Frankly, I can't see Houston ever assuming that role."

"I can," Paris said. "He actually watched Luke for me a couple of times when I had a meeting with the lodge's contractor. He didn't seem flustered at all, and had he been in town more, I'm sure he would have babysat whenever I asked."

Jill tried to picture Houston with an infant, without success. "I'm glad to know he has that side to him, but it doesn't quite gel with the whole tough-guy persona."

Paris waved at a middle-aged woman seated in the corner of the restaurant before bringing her attention back to Jill. "You know what they say. Don't judge a book by its cover, or in this case, a cowboy by his bull riding."

She recognized that in many ways, she had misjudged him over the past two years. He'd proven he was more than an irritable, injured rodeo rider. She'd even seen a few signs he had a wicked sense of humor and an inherent sensuality. Granted, she hadn't let herself see him in any other light to maintain professionalism. But now that he wasn't her patient, she'd begun to open her eyes. "I guess we're all guilty of prejudging people before we get to know them. My mother has the market cornered on that, though."

"Mine, too, at times," Paris said with a smile. "Tell me something, Jill. How are things between you and Houston?"

Jill swallowed hard. "What do you mean?"

"I mean he's a great-looking guy, and you're two consenting adults. You're staying in his guest room and—"

"Not after today," Jill interjected. "The apartment furniture is going to be delivered this afternoon."

"True, but that still leaves the past two nights in that big house, all alone with a hunk. I know it's really none of my business, but is there any chance you two might be experiencing a little chemistry?"

Had they ever. "What makes you think something like that would be possible?"

"Because you're a beautiful woman, and I know how irresistible the Calloway brothers can be. It took me less than one kiss with Dallas before I was ready to follow him anywhere. If you're attracted to Houston, and he's attracted to you, which I suspect he is, you should go for it."

Jill could use a sounding board, even if she didn't necessarily agree with Paris's advice. "If some chemistry is brewing between us, and I'm not saying it is, I don't believe it would be professional to act on it since we'll be working together as colleagues."

"Nonsense," Paris said. "Dallas hired me to design the lodge on the condition I marry him so he wouldn't lose control of the ranch, thanks to some ridiculous terms in his dad's will. We tossed professionalism out the window before the ink dried on our license."

She recalled Jenny mentioning that little tidbit, minus the dirty details. "So you didn't exactly go the traditional route, huh?"

"Not hardly. We met, married and then fell in love. Ass backward, as Dallas likes to say."

"I'm glad it worked out for you and Dallas, Paris, but I don't see Houston and I having that sort of relationship."

Paris narrowed her eyes and stared at her. "You don't see it or you're fighting it?"

Clearly Jill had guilt stamped on her face. "All right, I'm fighting it. For many reasons. First of all, I'm fairly sure Dallas wouldn't approve."

"He doesn't," Paris interjected. "He's not happy you've been bunking down at Houston's house. But he doesn't have any room to talk for all the reasons I cited earlier about our start in life together. Besides, I'll handle him if anything with you and Houston arises, if you catch my drift."

Jill sighed. "I've never been that spontaneous. Aside from taking a career path against my parents' wishes, I've almost always walked the straight and narrow. I've never engaged in sex for the sake of sex." Never really engaged in it, period.

"Well, maybe it's time you take the chance, Jill.

Take a little seduction out for a spin. You have a good start with those dresses you bought for the wedding. Houston's going to flip when he sees you in them."

So would her mother, Jill acknowledged. "I'm not sure seducing Houston is such a hot idea."

Paris grinned. "Oh, it could be very hot. And you shouldn't hesitate to take care of your needs with a man you know you can trust."

Aha! A personal reference. "How do I know I can trust him?"

Paris leaned over and patted her hand. "Because he's a Calloway brother, and they've been taught well when it comes to how to treat a woman. They have their mothers to thank for that."

Not exactly what she'd been led to believe. "According to Houston, Worth and Tyler are both serious players. And Houston enjoyed that reputation on the rodeo circuit."

"They're all charming to a fault, yet always respectful," Paris said. "Of course, their father was charming, too, but a total failure in the chivalry department. I believe that was also a contributing factor to their strong sense of honor. Heck, most of their former girlfriends still speak highly of them, to hear Maria tell it. Therefore, I can honestly say I believe Houston would never intentionally do anything to hurt you."

Maybe not physically, but he could damage her emotionally. If she let him. Which she wouldn't.

Jill had a lot to consider, and only a few days to do it before she might find herself spending an entire weekend with Houston at a wedding. Fortunately, she would be able to spend that time without him and assess if "going for it," as Paris had suggested, would be the best course or one massive mistake.

Seven

This whole "fake boyfriend" idea could very well wind up being one major mistake.

Houston determined that when, with less than a half hour until their scheduled landing in Florida and meeting of the parents, Jill still looked as nervous as a cat on a car radiator. "Are you going to be okay?"

She shot Houston a look that said she didn't appreciate the question. "I'm fine."

Yeah, right. "You look like you're about to jump out of your skin. Are you regretting having me with you?"

"No. I just don't like turbulence."

He recalled a couple of bumps, but that was it. "You're worried about facing your folks with me in tow."

She glanced away. "Maybe."

"No *maybe* about it. You've barely spoken a word since we boarded the plane. That was over two hours ago."

"I've been mentally rehearsing how I'm going to explain you."

"Apparently you've been doing that all week. I've barely seen you for more than a few minutes."

"I've been busy picking out furniture, stocking the kitchen, dress shopping with Paris, not to mention ordering first-aid supplies and all the medical equipment. You know, part of the job Dallas hired me to do?"

He didn't want a countdown of her activities. He wanted an explanation. Besides, she'd left going out of her way to ignore him from the list, and now that she'd moved out of his guest room, he'd found he missed the company. *Her* company. But he had all weekend to make up for lost time, before they returned to the reality of the ranch and she went back to ignoring him again.

Jill raked her gaze down his T-shirt and jeans and boots, a fair exchange since he'd been eyeing her short blue sleeveless dress since he'd picked her up this morning. Man, what he wouldn't give to run his hand underneath it. Or take it off completely.

"Did you bring any formal clothing?" she asked, disrupting his dirty thoughts.

"Yeah, a suit and a tux. Wasn't sure how fancy this shindig was going to be."

"You'll need both, the suit for the rehearsal dinner tonight at the country club and the tuxedo for the wedding tomorrow."

He narrowed his eyes and studied her head-on. "What would you have done if I hadn't brought either?"

She shrugged. "Winston would have taken you shopping."

He'd had a blue tick hound by that name at one time. "Who the hell is Winston?"

"You'll meet him soon enough."

The plane jolted, causing Jill to dig her nails into his arm, right above the cast. "We're in for some rocky weather," Frank said over the loudspeaker. "Just make sure you stay belted in. Shouldn't last too long."

"Great," Jill muttered. "A late summer storm. A sign of what's to come, I'm sure."

He patted her hand still clamped to his arm. "Stay calm. Cowboy Frank knows what he's doing."

She finally released her grip and sighed. "I was referring to the storm we're sure to encounter when you meet my mother, Hurricane Helen."

He'd deal with the fallout when the time came, even if he had to bring out his charm arsenal. "You haven't said a whole lot about your dad."

She leaned back against the headrest. "He's a good man. He rolls with the flow while my mother runs roughshod over him. He likes to keep the peace."

His own dad had been inclined to disturb the peace, but he'd always treated everyone fairly...except when it came to Maria and Jen. He'd totally screwed them around.

Jill straightened and leaned forward. "Do you have any white wine at the bar?"

"Sure." He released the belt and stood. "I'll get it."

"Not now," she said. "There's still lightning outside. Wait until we're sure the turbulence is over."

He figured it had only begun and might continue throughout the weekend. "Sweetheart, I've spent a lot of time sitting on top of mean, two-ton animals and their only goal is to throw me on my ass. I can handle a moving aisle."

"All right, tough guy."

"Glad you see it my way."

He sidestepped to the small refrigerator, opened the door, leaned over and located the miniature bottle of chardonnay, a staple they'd kept stocked for Jen. After uncapping it, he poured the wine into a plastic stem cup and returned to his seat without incident.

"Here you go," he said as he handed her the flute and a cocktail napkin. "A little liquid courage. Peanuts or pretzels to go with that drink?"

"No, thanks. Aren't you going to have anything?"

"Nope. It's not even noon yet."

She checked her watch. "I totally forgot the time."

He stretched out his legs and laced his hands on his belly. "Don't worry about the time. Your secret's safe with me."

She sipped the wine and smiled. "All of my secrets, I hope, are safe with you."

His mind reeled back to the night on the sofa,

and the liplock by the pool. "If you're talking about what happened between us a few days ago, I don't kiss and tell."

"At least that last time it was on you, not me."

She'd been all up against him, and that he hadn't been able to forget. "You enjoyed it and you know it."

"It was okay."

That might've offended him if she hadn't been lying. "Women don't moan when it's only okay."

She took a long drink of the wine this time. "I did not moan."

"Maybe it was more like a purr."

"I don't purr, either."

"Yeah, you do." And he wanted to know how she sounded when they really got down to business. He could forget about that right now because the chances that would happen were slim to none.

Jill downed the rest of the chardonnay and handed him the cup. "I'll have one more please."

"Do you think it's a good idea to show up on your mother's doorstep three sheets to the wind?"

She grinned. "Couldn't hurt, but I'm not going to get drunk on two glasses of wine. Relaxed maybe, but not intoxicated."

Her attitude put him in a not-so-great position. "I could refuse to serve you for your own good."

"Then I'll get it myself."

He didn't want her lack of judgment to come back to haunt him, but under normal circumstances, the alcohol content in wine wouldn't likely get a sparrow drunk. Even so, she was a self-proclaimed lightweight in the booze department. "Go ahead, but don't say I didn't warn you."

Jill looked perfectly steady when she slid out of the seat. Houston, on the other hand, felt a little lightheaded when the hem on that fitted dress rode high up her thighs as she crouched down in front of the fridge. "I don't see it."

He streaked both hands down his face. "It's in the shelf in the door."

"Oh, there it is."

Yeah, there it was—a woman who had him feeling hot and bothered. To make matters worse, when she started to work her way past him, the plane lurched and Jill landed the hand not holding the wine on his upper thigh. "Sorry," she said as she straightened. "That could have been a disaster if I'd spilled this all over you."

It could have been real revealing if she'd moved her palm a little higher. He wasn't the least bit worried about flying through a storm. He worried he might meet his demise if he didn't get some relief soon. Death by permanent woody.

"What's so funny?" Jill asked when she reclaimed her seat.

He hadn't realized he'd been smiling. "Not a thing. I was just thinking about how impressed I am you landed on your feet. You should try riding a bull sometime."

"Don't hold your breath."

He couldn't resist challenging her. "You're right. You're not tough enough."

She drank more wine and laid a dramatic hand above her breasts. "Someone release those orange butter cups from the ceiling. The cabin's filling up with testosterone and I need some oxygen."

He laughed to keep from groaning. "You beat all I've ever seen."

"Well, I try. Believe me, I'm surrounded by testosterone-ridden cowboys on a regular basis. It usually doesn't faze me."

"Usually?"

"It didn't until I've gotten to know you better."

His ego puffed up like a rooster in a henhouse. "Is that bad or good?"

"I'm not sure. I mean, you're not my type. Frankly, I don't have a type. I really haven't had enough of a social life over the past few years to find out."

"Only you can change that by getting out there and taking a few chances."

"You're right." After finishing off the wine, she leaned over him and set the glass on the counter, putting them too close for Houston's comfort. "But I could use some help."

He could, too, he realized, after she brushed up against him. "What kind of help?"

"Well—"

"Tie yourself down, folks" boomed from the overhead speaker. "We'll be on the ground shortly."

They both secured their seat belts before Jill continued. "I've decided to take this weekend and be less guarded, more carefree. Stop listening to my mother's warnings. Throw caution to the wind."

Houston had no idea what that entailed, but he was damn sure going to find out. "What exactly does that mean ? Aside from showing up tipsy for the nuptials."

She playfully slapped at his arm. "I'm not tipsy, and before I answer your question, I have one for you. Would you say we have chemistry?"

His body had been telling him that for almost a week, loud and clear. "Yeah. You could say that."

"Good. I thought it was just me."

"Are you serious? It's all I can do not to climb all over you whenever you walk in the room."

Her eyes went wide. "Seriously?"

"Well, yeah. Could you not tell that when I kissed you by the pool? Or when you kissed me?"

"Look, Houston, I'm not naive. I just don't have a lot of experience when it comes to male-female relationship dynamics."

He'd gathered that, but he couldn't believe she didn't see in herself what he saw in her. "You're a beautiful, sexy woman. Any man would be crazy not to want to be with you."

"Yes, they're all lined up at my door back at the ranch."

She honestly didn't get it. "Don't forget that my brothers almost came to blows over who was going to escort you here."

She smiled. "Until you intervened."

"Yep. I wasn't going to have those two hounds dogging you the entire weekend."

"You're not going to dog me?"

Not if he could help it, though that was up in the air at the moment. "I'm not going to do anything you don't want to do."

"Would you kiss me again if I asked?"

"Yeah."

"Would you touch me if I asked?"

Oh, hell yeah. "Anywhere you want me to touch you."

When the plane began to descend, Houston figured the conversation would have to continue on the ride to her house. Jill had other ideas.

"Before we land, there is one thing I have to tell you," she said.

He could only guess what that might be. "Shoot."

"When I said I've had little experience with men, I should have said I've had no measurable experience."

Houston's mind began to reel over the implication. No way. No how. Not a gorgeous woman like her. "Are you telling me—"

"I'm saying, to use an antiquated term, that for all intents and purposes, I'm a virgin."

To say Houston still looked stunned would be a major understatement. Jill had less than ten minutes to bring him out of his stupor before they met the welcoming committee. Fortunately Winston had closed the partition dividing the Bentley's front and back seats, allowing them some privacy. "I know this little tidbit has come as quite a surprise, but—"

"You could say that. I don't know many women who haven't taken that step by the time they're in their midtwenties. Heck, I don't believe I know *any* women who haven't had sex before." He reached over the console and took her hand. "All this means is you're discriminating when it comes to men. And for that reason it scares the hell out of me to even consider us having some kind of weekend fling. You deserve better."

She deserved to make that decision on her own. "I don't have any expectations, Houston, other than having a good time. If anything happens between us, I accept that we'll go back to being friends and occasional adversaries."

He remained silent for a time before asking, "Why me? Aside from the chemistry thing."

"I've asked myself that quite a bit. The answer is I'm sure you know what you're doing, and I can trust you to respect me."

"Just so you know, I don't take any of this lightly. My mother has always told me that women are to be treated well. My father showed me how if you ignore that, you only create heartache. I don't want that to happen to you."

Exactly what Paris had told her. "In your estimation, I might not be tough enough to ride a bull, but I'm emotionally stronger than you realize."

"How do you know how you're going to feel if you've never had sex before?"

"I'm not totally innocent, Houston. I've been on dates with guys who had roving hands."

"And none of them succeeded in getting you into bed?"

She refused to believe he was that obtuse, only amazed. "A few tried, all failed. It never really felt right."

"But you honestly think it would be right between us?"

"As hard as it is to believe, yes, I do. And I do because I'm not that college student anymore. I have needs and I want to explore all the possibilities. But if you're not willing—"

"I didn't say that."

Her optimism began to climb. "Then you will consider it? No pressure, of course."

He seemed to mull it over for a few moments before he responded. "I'll consider it, but only on one condition."

Her optimism threatened to fall off the cliff. "What would that be?"

"If we get into some of this exploring, and you want to back out, you only have to tell me and it's over."

She didn't foresee that happening. But then she hadn't predicted she would ever ask him for some sensual attention. "That's fair."

When the car slowed, Jill glanced out the window and realized they were pulling into the lengthy drive. "Looks like we've arrived at the esteemed Amherst estate."

"Then I guess it's time to start the show." He tipped her face toward him and smiled. "Want to get in a little practice?"

"Do you really have to ask?"

"Yeah, I do. I want to make sure you haven't changed your mind."

"In two minutes?"

"Stranger things have happened."

Yes, as in she'd propositioned him. Her mother would be so proud. "I would like nothing better than to engage in a little lip practice with you."

He kissed her then, softly at first, then more deeply. She was so engrossed in the moment, she didn't realize they'd stopped, or that Winston had opened the door. She didn't realize they had an audience, either, until she heard the familiar voice.

"Oh, my stars, Jillian Elizabeth, why on earth are you kissing that cowboy?"

Eight

Jill abruptly ended the kiss and leaned around Houston to discover her mother on the top step beneath the portico, standing as stiff as her strawberry blond bob hairdo and sporting her patent disapproving look.

After leaning back against the seat again, Jill muttered, "Hurricane Helen is about to be unleashed. Let the destruction begin."

Houston sent a quick glance in her mother's direction. "How does she even know I'm a cowboy when I'm not wearing my hat?"

"Big silver belt buckle, jeans and boots. Dead giveaway."

"Hadn't thought about that."

Jill wondered what he thought about the queen of the manor. In light of Helen's glare, he probably wished he hadn't agreed to come. "Climb on out and let's get this over with. And it's best if initially you let me do all the talking."

"Whatever you say."

After Houston exited the Bentley, he offered his hand and helped Jill out. She adjusted her dress and walked right up to Helen with the cowboy in residence trailing behind her. "Hello, Mother."

"You haven't answered my question." She pointed a finger at Houston. "Who is this man?"

Jill glanced back as if she'd forgotten he was there. "Oh. Him. I picked him up on the way from the airport." She clasped Houston's cast-wrapped hand and lifted it up. "He was hitchhiking. You couldn't miss the thumb."

Helen's mouth gaped open. "You picked up a stranger? Winston, what were you thinking?" she shouted at the driver now bent over the trunk, unloading the bags.

The white-haired, goatee-bedecked family fixture leaned around the car and smiled at Jill. "I was only following Miss Jillian's instructions."

Time to set the record straight before Winston found himself in the unemployment line. "I'm not serious, Mother. This is my guest. He's also my... my..."

"I'm her fiancé." While Jill froze on the spot, Houston offered his good hand to Helen, which she promptly ignored. "Houston Calloway. Pleasure to meet you, ma'am."

Fiancé? This time Jill was a victim of the verbal

stun gun. So much for Houston letting her do all the talking. Oh, joy. She might as well play along. What better way to thwart her mother's usual matchmaking? "Yes, mother, meet your future son-in-law."

Helen continued to disregard Houston's extended hand and turned her ire on Jill. "You might have said something when we spoke last. I had no idea you were dating anyone, much less engaged to a man we've never met."

Houston wrapped his arm around Jill's shoulder and gave her a squeeze. "It was kind of a spontaneous proposal, ma'am. Or maybe I should start calling you Mom?"

Helen looked no less unhappy over the situation. "Mrs. Amherst would be best since I don't know you at all."

"Works for me for now," Houston said with a grin. "Once you get to know me, you're gonna love me."

"Houston asked me to marry him while we were on the plane," Jill interjected. "I was very surprised."

"Yeah, she was, and real excited." He looked at her and winked before bringing his attention back to her mother. "I still don't have a ring yet, but we'll take care of that soon. Unless you have some kind of family heirloom you want her to have. That sure would save me some time and money."

Helen lifted her chin. "No, I do not. And I would prefer you not mention any of this to your father right away. His health hasn't been too good of late."

Jill felt a bite of panic. "What's wrong?"

"His heart," her mother replied nonchalantly.

"I don't remember you mentioning *that* to me when you called, Mother."

She waved a hand in dismissal. "He doesn't want anyone to make a fuss. Now come this way, but take care not to disrupt the wedding planner's staff." She sent a pointed look at Houston's feet. "And please wipe your boots on the mat. They polished the marble this morning."

Houston tipped an imaginary hat. "Yes, ma'am."

They walked through the foyer and into a flurry of activity. One woman was draping greenery and white flowers on the banister while a man moved around her mother's prized furniture in the parlor to their left. Houston and Jill followed Helen past the library and into the den at the rear of the house, the only living space where Jill had ever felt comfortable. All the antique settees and chairs and expensive accessories had never held any appeal.

When Helen said, "I'll return shortly," and started toward the kitchen, Jill showed Houston to the white leather sectional, where they sat side by side.

He draped his arm over the back of the sofa and surveyed the most comfortable room, aside from the all-white color pallet. "Nice digs."

"Nice job of acting," Jill said in a lowered voice. "I can't believe you actually told her we're engaged. What were you thinking?"

"Sorry. It kind of shot out of my mouth when she kept looking at me like I was pond sludge."

Jill couldn't contain her smile when she remembered her mother's reaction. "The shock on her face was kind of amusing. You're one of the few people to ever put her in her place."

"When do you want to tell her the truth?"

She had to think about that for a moment. "Not until after we're ready to return to the ranch. After I reveal all, we'll need to make a quick escape."

"Good plan. You can tell her we broke up when you found out I don't have a dime to my name."

"Or that you already have a wife and kids." Mortification rushed through Jill when she realized what she'd said. "I'm so, so sorry. That was insensitive in light of your father's history."

"Don't sweat it. It's not that big of a deal anymore."

She surmised that attitude was the product of self-preservation. "Anyway, I appreciate your covering for me in such a creative way."

Houston chuckled. "You can thank me later, sweet cakes."

Sweet cakes? "You're welcome, honey bun. And whatever you do, don't tell her you have money."

"Sure thing."

"Don't mention a word about the new job."

"Not a problem, and don't worry, I can handle Helen. You ain't seen nothing yet."

Jill was left to speculate about his intentions when her mother reentered the room holding two crystal glasses. She set coasters in front of them and placed the drinks atop the copper disks.

"I took the liberty of serving you some of Penelope's famous raspberry tea," Helen said as she pulled up the club chair closer to the sofa. "I assume you like tea, Mr. Calloway."

He shrugged. "Call me Houston, and tea will do, unless you have a beer. Or whiskey."

Her mother looked slightly appalled. "We don't serve alcohol this time of day."

Jill found it amusing that Helen had discounted her three-martini lunches with the bridge club, a fact she decided not to point out.

Houston planted his palm above Jill's knee. "Then tea it is."

Helen eyed his hand before raising her condescending gaze to his. "Tell me, Mr. Calloway. What do you do for a living?"

"Well, Helen, I pretty much herd cows and slop pigs. Tend to the horse, that kind of thing."

Her mother looked as if she'd eaten a pickle. "Then you live on a ranch?"

"Yes, ma'am. A working cattle ranch in deep South Texas."

"It's an hour south of San Antonio," Jill said.

"And about seventy miles from the Mexican border," Houston added. "The livestock pretty much outnumber the people in those parts."

Helen's green eyes went wide. "Jillian, where on earth are you going to work if you're in the middle of nowhere?"

"I'm not sure yet."

"She doesn't have to work," Houston said. "Except for maybe feeding the chickens."

Jill scraped her brain for a way to end the inquisition before they dug a deeper deception trench. "Where's Daddy?"

"Outside. Are you certain you're cut out for ranching life, Jillian?"

So much for the subject-changing tact. "Actually, I—"

"Sure she is," Houston broke in. "She's one tough little lady. And as far as making her own money goes, she doesn't need to. I don't have much, but I do have a two-bedroom house and enough money to put food on the table and raise a passel of babies."

And Jill hadn't thought her mother could look any more stunned. "A passel of babies?" Helen repeated.

"Yes, ma'am. At least four, maybe five." Houston popped a kiss on Jill's cheek. "I like to keep my women barefoot and pregnant."

Helen eyed him suspiciously. "Your *women*?"

"Woman," Houston corrected. "There's only one woman for me, and that's this little gal here."

If he squeezed her any tighter, Jill might actually wince. "Any other questions, Mother?"

"I'm sure I will think of more as the weekend wears on."

The sound of footsteps drew everyone's attention to the den's entry. When Jill spotted him, she instantly hopped off the sofa and rushed to him. "Hi, Daddy!"

He pulled her into a long hug before taking a step back. "My, my, ladybug, you're still as pretty as ever."

Jill noticed he wore his traditional white tennis clothes and she found that disturbing. "Dad, are you sure you should be on the court considering your heart issues?"

"I don't have heart problems. I have acid reflux."

They both shot a look in Helen's direction before Jill said, "Mother told me—"

"Don't listen to your mother, ladybug. She exaggerates everything."

"I don't necessarily believe your doctors, Benjamin," Helen said. "They barely ran any tests."

"They ran every test known to humankind," her father retorted before spying Houston. "Who is this young man?"

Houston stood, stepped forward and extended his hand for a shake. "Houston Calloway, sir. I'm Jill's—"

"Friend," Jill added.

"He's her fiancé," Helen stated with a good deal of disdain in her tone.

She hated lying to her father and decided to set him straight when they had a moment alone. "Mother didn't want us to mention it—she led us to believe you might have a cardiac arrest."

"Ignore your mother's flair for the dramatic. This is very welcome news." He gave Houston's hand a hearty shake. "Welcome to the family, son. Just don't tell me you plan to marry tomorrow. One wedding in this house is quite enough."

Jill would wholeheartedly agree to that. "Don't be concerned, Dad. Houston and I plan to have a long engagement."

Houston frowned. "Aw, now, sweetheart. I'm thinking the quicker we get married, the better."

Helen's eyes went wide. "What does he mean by that, Jillian? Are you expecting?"

She was expecting to have the lies come back to bite her on the backside, but she resented her mother drawing that conclusion. "Why, Mom? No one would ask me to marry them if I wasn't?"

"That's not what I'm saying," Helen retorted. "I believe we have a right to know if our daughter is pregnant out of wedlock."

At the moment, Jill had no desire to correct her mother's supposition. "We'll discuss it later. Right now we'd like to get settled in."

"Where shall I put these, Miss Jillian?"

Jill looked beyond her father to see Winston hauling the luggage into the den. But before she could respond, her mother popped out of the chair and said, "Jillian will be staying in her sister's room. Mr. Calloway will be in the pool house, unless he's arranged for a hotel room."

"Nope," Houston said. "I'm a little short on cash, but I could find a cheap motel if I'm going to be putting you out."

Ben patted Houston on the back. "Nonsense, son. You're part of the family now."

Jill had one burning question to pose. "What's wrong with me staying in my old room?"

"It's been turned into a guest room," Helen began, "and we have guests occupying every suite. You and

Pamela can share her room for a night and get re-acquainted."

She'd rather eat garden sod. Jill also refused to allow her mother to dictate the sleeping arrangements. "I'll be staying in the pool house, as well, Winston."

Helen looked mortified. "You certainly will not, Jillian. It only has one bedroom."

"If you seriously believe I'm pregnant, and I'm not saying I am, why can't I stay with Houston? I can't get knocked up twice."

Helen lifted her chin and folded her arms tightly across her middle. "Pregnant or not, it wouldn't be proper."

"Come on now, Helen," Jill's father chimed in. "They're adults. I recall a time or ten when you and I occupied the same room before we married, and we know how that turned out."

Helen crossed her arms tightly and huffed. "That is not going to happen beneath my roof, Benjamin. End of story."

Her dad sent Jill a sympathetic look. "Sorry, ladybug. The hurricane has spoken, and considering her stress level, it's best not to unleash her."

Jill nixed further protests out of respect for her father. Besides, she could still find a way to spend the evening with Houston without anyone's knowledge. "Fine." She turned to Winston. "If you'll just take the blue luggage upstairs, I'll show Houston to the pool house."

"As you wish, Miss Jillian."

When Jill turned back to her mother, she sensed another lecture coming on and quelled it immediately. "Before you say anything, I assure you the sanctity of the pool house will remain intact." For the next few hours. "What time is the dinner tonight?"

"Seven o'clock sharp," Helen said. "Do you have an appropriate dress for the event?"

"Yes. Red-and-white gingham with matching ruby-red shoes. Grab your luggage and follow me, *fiancé*."

She heard Houston chuckling while he gathered his bags and followed her as she marched through the sun room. When she headed out the doors that led to the pool deck, she spotted a huge white tent in the distance, set up near the lake.

"So that's where the magic is going to happen," Houston said from behind her.

"Yes. It's a nice backdrop for a wedding."

"I meant the pool house."

This time she laughed. "I suppose that remains to be seen."

He came to her side and matched her steps. "You can always sneak out after everyone's gone to bed."

Clearly he'd read her mind back in the house. "Provided my mother doesn't post a guard at my sister's bedroom door."

"I could always climb up and carry you out the window."

"Banner idea. I'll have Winston fetch a ladder."

She opened the door to the blue-and-white cottage, expecting to see that the decor hadn't changed since she'd left home. In reality, it had. The furnishings had all been updated in muted tones of white and gray with a pop of lime green in places. She assumed they'd renovated it when they'd turned her room into guest quarters. As much as she hated to admit it, that stung like a hornet and only cemented how far removed she'd become from her family.

"This will work just fine," Houston said as he stepped inside.

"It's nice enough." Jill walked to the bedroom and surveyed the space. "I'm not sure how much you're going to like this."

Houston slid his arms around her from behind. "Haven't seen that since I shared a room with Tyler when we were kids."

"Those twin beds are a monument to my mother's contempt for all things sexual."

"Yeah, I figured that out pretty quickly. I can't figure out why you didn't deny the whole baby thing."

"Hey, you set it up by adding that whole 'the quicker the better' thing."

"I figured she'd just think I couldn't wait to make you my bride. I didn't know she'd actually go straight to the baby thing."

"Of course she would, and for all the reasons I stated to her." She looked back at him and grinned. "That said, it was kind of cool to get engaged and pregnant in less than an hour."

He was uncharacteristically quiet for a few moments. "Have you ever talked to your mom about her attitude?"

She faced him and thought back to her formative years. "No. She did all the talking."

"Maybe you should broach that subject while you're here."

"Why?"

"Because people who have negative opinions about sex usually have something in their past that's influenced them."

He'd made a good point that she should seriously contemplate. "If the sex subject comes up before the end of the weekend, and I'm sure it will, I'll consider addressing it then, when I tell her there's no baby or impending wedding."

"Good idea." He pulled her into his arms. "You don't hold sex in contempt, do you?"

She shook her head and swallowed hard. "Fortunately it doesn't appear to be genetic."

"Damn fortunate." He brushed his lips across her forehead. "This cowpoke would sure like to kiss this lady."

"This lady would like to be kissed."

He lowered his head and paused. "You don't think they have surveillance cameras in here, do you?"

"Knowing Helen, it's entirely possible. However, my father would draw the line at voyeurism."

"Good to know."

As Houston kissed her soundly, Jill put all her concerns about family issues away. She didn't care about the sleeping arrangements or enduring social events with pretentious people. She only cared about Houston's hands roving down her back, the undeniable heat when he backed her against the wall and pressed against her. She couldn't claim she wasn't surprised, and excited, when his hand came to rest on her breast. She was also taken aback by her immediate reaction to his touch when he used his fingertips to work her nipple into a tight knot. His skill told her this wasn't his first time at first base. Not exactly her first time, either, but he'd obviously been playing the game for some time.

When Houston breezed his lips down her neck and began toying with the back zipper, Jill reacted with a little shudder and a bit of caution. With a bedroom so close, she recognized how easy it would be give in to sexual oblivion. But with her parents nearby, they would be risking discovery.

"What are you doing, Houston Calloway?" she said in a raspy tone.

"I want to take off this dress, and it's damn sure not because I want to borrow it."

She wanted him to take it off. Honestly, she did, but... "Do think now is the right time with my mother lurking in the shadows?"

"Probably not." He released his hold on her, moved to one side and tipped his forehead against the wall. "I'm so jacked up right now I could take you right here. But this isn't how I want your first time to be."

The fact he'd considered her feelings, and not the prospect of getting caught, buoyed her spirits. "I appreciate that," she said as she readjusted her clothing. "Although in reality, I wouldn't have objected to a little more foreplay."

He straightened and half grinned, half groaned. "Darlin', if you want foreplay, just wait for what I have in store for you tonight."

While Houston waited next to the white limo, he wasn't sure what to expect tonight. Rubbing elbows with a bunch of stuck-up people wasn't his idea of a good time. Country music and barn dances were more his style. But for Jill's sake, he'd make do and be a perfect gentleman. He'd behave himself in public and keep his hands to himself. No one would ever know that getting Jillian in his bed, even a twin bed, would be first and foremost on his mind.

That plan was pretty much shot to hell when Jill emerged from the mansion wearing a low-cut, little black dress and matching high heels, her hair piled high on her head, leaving her neck fair game. But the way she looked at the moment—a little pissed off—probably meant she had no desire to make out in the back seat of a moving vehicle.

After the driver opened the door, Jill slid inside and he claimed the spot beside her. Houston questioned why they didn't immediately move. "Are we waiting for someone else?"

Jill crossed her legs, inadvertently hiking up her hem. "No, thank heavens. We're the last to leave."

"Bad day?"

"Boring day. How about you?"

"I watched a little baseball, took a little nap. Oh, and Penelope brought me a tray of sandwiches."

"Were they good?"

Not nearly as good as Jill looked, and smelled. "They were about as big as my banged-up thumb, but they were okay. They had some kind of cream cheese stuff and, best of all, no poison."

She finally smiled. "Lucky for me."

He shrugged out of the jacket and tossed it on the seat across from him. If he had his way, that wouldn't be the only article of clothing coming off tonight. "How did it go with your sister?"

"It didn't. She was flitting about the house and, when she saw me, muttered a greeting, then went out to the tent for the wedding run-through."

"Did you go?"

"I didn't feel the need to rehearse sitting in the audience."

He immediately noticed the bitterness in her tone. "You didn't see her when you were getting ready tonight?"

She shook her head. "No. Apparently she decided to dress at her maid of honor's hotel room. I'm sure alcohol was involved, which could be interesting during this little soiree."

Doing what he wanted to do to her, right then and there, could be damn interesting. He decided to be subtle, not come on too strong. For those reasons, he laid his palm above her knee.

"You look real pretty tonight, ma'am."

"You look nice, too. Very handsome. You clean up good, Calloway."

Maybe so, but he was having some fairly dirty thoughts. "How many people are attending this dinner?"

When he drew slow circles on the inside of her leg, she released a ragged sigh. "I'd guess a hundred or so of my mother's closest friends."

He let his fingertip drift upward, but not too far. "I like an intimate gathering."

"I like…"

"You'd like what, darlin'?"

She closed her eyes and her legs opened slightly. "Um… I'm not sure."

He pressed a kiss on her temple. "How are you feeling right now?"

"Very warm."

"Want me to tell the driver to turn up the air-conditioning?"

Her eyes snapped open and she frowned. "I'm not exactly *that* kind of hot."

He ran his palm up the inside of her thigh. "Oh, yeah?"

"Oh, yeah."

"You feeling a little turned on tonight?"

Without verbally responding, she wrapped her hand around his neck and pulled his mouth to hers for a long, deep kiss. "Does that answer your question?"

"Pretty much."

Considering that kiss his cue to continue, he

leaned over and grabbed his coat, then draped it across her lap. Awareness dawned in her expression, and she shuddered when he slid his hand back beneath her skirt.

Houston rimmed the edge of her panties with his fingertip, and really wanted that scrap of lace gone. But before he did that, he decided to test the waters by pressing his palm between her legs. He encountered a good deal of dampness and heat. And after just a couple of strokes in a prime place, Jill made a small sound in her throat, grabbed his arm and shook like the devil.

Without much effort on his part, she'd gone off like a rocket. Even though it pleased him to know he'd given her some pleasure, he was seriously feeling the effects.

Jill leaned back against the seat and muttered, "Wow," right when the car pulled up to the country club's front door behind several more sedans. "I didn't expect that to happen."

He kissed her cheek. "Neither did I, sweetheart. But your quick-to-fire reaction isn't all that surprising."

"The pitfalls of celibacy." She smiled but it quickly went away. "This isn't at all fair to you."

"I'll be fine, if you give me a few minutes."

She sent a pointed look at his groin. "Oh. I see."

His predicament was hard to miss. "Yep. Unless you want me to be the sideshow at dinner, we're going to have to sit here a little longer."

Jill looked out the rear window. "We don't have

much longer, but I have an idea." She brought her focus back to him. "Just think about the fact that you're going to be hanging out with Hurricane Helen all night."

He'd be damned if that didn't do the trick.

Houston felt secure enough to put on his jacket in preparation for a night with the presumed in-laws. He figured if he could take on a rank bull, he could handle the Amherst family. Besides, he was more than curious to meet Jill's sister.

When they finally worked their way inside the entrance, he saw women in fine dresses and men with expensive watches. The net worth of this crowd had to be in the billions.

Jill slipped her arm through his, signaling the pretending had begun. She led him toward Ben and Helen, who were being greeted by several guests. He had no trouble spotting the bride-to-be. He noted only a slight resemblance to Jill. Her hair was much redder and she was a whole lot shorter. He'd classify her as fresh-faced pretty, where Jill was more refined and, yeah, elegant. She stood next to a tall, lanky guy with brown hair who kept looking at her like he'd won the prize.

As they waited for the crowd to clear, Houston's first impression of the couple happened to be they were damn young. His second—they actually looked real glad to be together. Maybe it was all just a front to please the folks. Or maybe he was too jaded to believe in ever-after. He had his own father to thank for that.

Jill began to move forward and murmured, "Time to put on our happy faces and get this over with."

Houston wanted to get it over with and get a beer, or a shot of whiskey. Probably the best whiskey money could buy. Free whiskey, in this case. Nothing wrong with that.

When Jill released his arm to hug her dad, Houston hung back and waited until he was properly introduced. Her hesitancy to embrace her mom wasn't lost on Houston, nor was the coolness when she greeted her sister. He wasn't the least bit surprised to see her shaking the groom's hand, like he was more stranger than longtime acquaintance. There was so much not-so-great history in the group that someone could write a family self-help book on the spot.

After Jill waved Houston over, Ben gave him a hearty handshake and Helen gave him a fake smile that caused the devil to land on his shoulder. He immediately pulled the female hurricane into a bear hug, and wished he had a camera to capture the stunned look on her face.

"Houston," Jill began, "this is my sister, Pamela. Pamela, my fiancé, Houston."

She didn't smile, didn't offer her hand, and that plain pissed him off. "Nice to finally meet you."

"Likewise," she said without a scrap of sincerity in her tone.

The groom stuck out his hand. "I'm Clark Hamilton," he said. "Helen told us you're a rancher."

Houston returned the gesture and said, "Yep. Born and bred Texan."

Clark grinned. "I envy you. I always wanted to live that cowboy lifestyle."

Pamela elbowed him in the side. "Be serious, Clark."

He frowned at his bride. "I am serious."

"It's a hard life," Houston said as he slipped his arm around Jill's waist. "But it has its rewards. Nothing better than a long day of working the land and coming home to a good woman."

Clark rubbed his jaw. "And you can make a decent living at it?"

If the guy only knew. "Yeah, if you're willing to take a few odd jobs when times get hard."

Houston then noticed a tall blonde woman with a phone standing nearby, several other young women gathered around her, staring at the screen. He couldn't imagine what all the fuss was about, until the blonde and her girlfriends made their way toward him.

"Excuse me," she said. "Are you Houston Calloway?"

Damn. His first instinct involved denial, and his second involved backing out the door. He figured it was too late for either. "Yeah."

"I told you that was him," she said to one of her friends. She then held up the screen to proudly display an internet ad featuring him. The one that had just shown up on billboards throughout the country. The one where he was shirtless with a blue compression band around his bicep. Oh, hell.

Houston turned to discover Ben looking a little

rattled and the happy couple looking more than a tad bit shocked.

And Hurricane Helen looked more than ready to blow as she faced her oldest daughter with a glare. "Jillian Elizabeth Amherst, why in heaven's name are you marrying a porn star?"

"I assure you, Dad, Houston is not a porn star."

Her father downed a shot of bourbon and patted her cheek. "I know that, ladybug. Are you really surprised your mother went there?"

Jill glanced from her seat at the bar to Helen, who was surrounded by a few of her favorite gossips, most likely doing damage control. "I guess I shouldn't be shocked. She has a way of making something as innocuous as an ad campaign into something lurid."

"That she does," he said. "And your young man might not be a porn star, but right now he looks like a rock star."

She followed her dad's gaze to Houston standing near the dance floor, a bevy of bridesmaids hanging on his every word. Unwelcome jealousy bit into her when she saw one petite blonde whispering something in his ear. "Do you think they're asking him to autograph their cell phones?"

"I think they're treading on your territory, ladybug. I also think you should walk over there right now and take it back."

Jill turned around and took a sip of wine, knowing full well she had no real claim on him. "He knows where I am. When he's finished with the fawning, he'll find me."

"Honey, he's your man, and you need to let him, and all those women, know that. Ask him to dance."

Heavens, she hadn't danced since her senior cotillion, and she wasn't sure she remembered how. "Houston doesn't seem like he cares to dance."

"He seems as if he'd like to be rescued. I've noticed him looking over here several times."

Jill glanced Houston's way and received a smile from him for the effort. "You're right, Dad. I'm going to march over there and reclaim my *man*." And if Houston took exception to the intrusion, too bad. He'd started the phoney fiancé scheme and she intended to keep it going.

After drinking the last of the chardonnay, Jill slid off the stool and hugged her father. She then strode across the room as fast as her heels would let her and walked right up to Houston. "Excuse me, honey, but I'm here to honor your request for that dance."

His expression said *What dance?*

"Sure. Now?"

She hooked her arm through his. "Yes, now. It's a lovely, romantic ballad. What better way to celebrate our love?" She sent a pointed look at the blonde who didn't seem pleased at the interruption. "So if you'll excuse us, ladies, I'm going to steal my fiancé for the rest of the evening."

As the women scattered, Houston led her onto the dance floor and regarded her again. "I'm more into country dancing, but I guess I can wing it."

"Just put your arms around me and move in time to the music. That's all there is to it."

But that wasn't all, she realized, when he pulled her close. As she rested her cheek against his chest, the warmth of his body, the hint of his clean-scent cologne, had a magical effect on her. The music continued to play, a slow, sultry romantic tune, Houston held her closer, pressed a kiss on her temple and for a moment Jill felt as if they were a real couple, falling in love.

Yet that was only a fantasy, and a farce. A show for the family's benefit, and it had done its job, Jill determined, when glanced to her left to see her mother and father looking on. Where Ben looked pleased, Helen looked skeptical. And not far away, she noticed Pamela and Clark dancing, too, only their affection seemed sincere. She predicted her sister would be pregnant in a matter of months, and that would make her Aunt Jill. An absentee aunt. Maybe the time had come to make amends with Pamela, or at least try. Question was, how did she erase all the years of resentment? How could she reconnect with a sibling she barely knew? Obstacles that she might not be able to overcome.

When Houston whispered, "Are you okay?" Jill realized she had tensed in his arms.

She relaxed a bit and met his worried gaze. "I'm fine. Just ready to get out of here."

"Looks like a lot of people already have."

When the song ended, Jill surveyed the room and realized the crowd had thinned quite a bit. "If we hurry, we might be able to claim a limo all to ourselves."

He brushed a kiss across her lips and grinned. "I'd be up for a little more limo foreplay."

"You're a bad, bad boy, Calloway."

"You're a damn sexy woman, Amherst. Now let's go before someone notices us leaving."

The minute Houston took Jill's hand and led her off the floor, she heard, "Ladybug, wait up."

Being the dutiful daughter, Jill faced her father with a smile. "We were just leaving, Dad."

"That's why I stopped you," he said. "Your mother insists on staying and conducting the postmortem on the event. In other words, discuss everyone ad nauseum with the bridge club. Personally, I want to go to bed, so do you mind if I accompany you?"

How could she say no? She sent Houston an apologetic look before saying, "Of course, Dad."

So much for canoodling in the car with her cowboy, but then again, they had all night to spend together.

Nine

Dressed in khaki shorts, gold sandals and a sleeveless coral blouse, Jill knocked on the pool house door and waited for Houston to answer the summons—if he hadn't already taken off for Texas.

A few seconds later, he opened the door wearing worn jeans and a T-shirt, no shoes and an unreadable expression. "Are you sure you want to be seen with a porn star?" he asked without a touch of amusement in his voice.

"Leave it to Helen to make that assumption," Jill muttered. "And I'm really sorry for any embarrassment she might have caused with her accusations."

"Not a problem. I've been called worse. Besides, I probably sold a few of those compression wraps in spite of the questionable PR."

At least his tone had lightened somewhat. "I think we've cleared everything up fairly well." Everything but the bogus engagement and presumed pregnancy. "However, I won't be a bit surprised to see several smitten bridesmaids sporting those wraps at the wedding in honor of the shirtless internet cowboy in attendance."

"I hope not," he said. "Helen would have my hide for messing up the dress code."

Speaking of Helen… "Do you mind if I come in before the troops come home and catch me sneaking out here to see you?"

He eyed the overnight bag in her hand. "Do you plan to stay awhile?"

A sudden bout of insecurity blanketed Jill, and she suddenly wondered if he'd changed his mind about the overnight due to the debacle. "Only if you'd like me to stay."

Finally, he smiled. A sexy, devious smile. "I can take you for a few hours, and you can take that any way you want."

The somewhat suggestive comment suddenly spurred Jill's confidence, and fantasies. "Sounds like a great way to spend the night."

"You bet it is."

The second Jill stepped inside, Houston reeled her into his arms and kissed her soundly but ended it all too soon. "I found a few beers in the fridge. Do you want something to drink?"

She had a sudden crazy craving. "Actually, I know what I want, but it's not a drink."

"Same here, but I thought we might wait a bit to make sure the family's all tucked into bed. Once I get started, I don't want any interruptions."

She set the bag on the nearby chair, stood on tip-toe and kissed his chin. "Actually, this has to do with dessert."

He winked. "Darlin', you can call it whatever you'd like."

"I'm referring to a literal dessert." She wrested herself from his grasp, strode to the fridge, opened the freezer and pulled out the treat before she faced him. "My mother's favorite, although she swears she doesn't eat them, hence hiding them away in the pool house."

"An ice cream pop?"

"Yes. Strawberries and cream, to be exact. It's the last one."

"Are you sure you want to take it then?"

"Of course. Why not?"

"Because you're gonna risk resurrecting the wrath of Helen if she finds a bare freezer."

"She can buy more, and frankly I'm in the mood to live a little dangerously."

"Has my risk taking rubbed off on you?"

"Not exactly, but the night is young, so we have plenty of time for rubbing." Without waiting for Houston's response, Jill crossed the room, sat on the couch and patted the spot beside her. "Come here and I'll share it with you."

Houston walked to the fridge to procure a beer. "I'll come there, but I don't need any ice cream." As soon as he dropped onto the sofa beside her, he said, "Now let's make a deal."

"What would that be?"

"We don't talk about what happened tonight."

"Are you referring to the unfortunate advertisement thing or the thing in the limo?"

"The advertisement thing, but I don't mind discussing the limo incident." He set the bottle down on the coffee table, rested his arm on the back of the sofa and laid his palm on her leg. "I figure we might want to reenact that scene a little later, this time without clothes."

Holy Toledo, what an image. "I might be game for that."

He frowned. "Might be?"

"Your odds are good." After pulling the protective paper from the ice cream, Jill sucked the rocket-shaped pop into her mouth, and for some reason, Houston grimaced. "What's wrong?"

His golden-brown eyes seemed to turn a shade darker. "Do you want me to be honest?"

She took another quick lick. "Sure."

"I'm thinking it would be a whole lot easier on me if your mother's favorite dessert was a piece of cake, not a frozen ice bomb on a stick. Watching you putting your mouth on it is making me damn hot and real bothered."

Awareness dawned when her gaze came to rest on the obvious bulge below his waistband. "Oh, I see."

He shifted on the cushion. "I'm sure you probably do. It's kind of obvious."

"Just a little bit."

Feeling wild and somewhat wicked, Jill laid the ice cream on the wrapper resting on the table, then straddled Houston's lap. He sent her a grin that shamed the stars. "Lady, are you trying to drive me crazy?"

"Yes. Is it working?"

"I'm about as close to the edge as I can be without falling over the cliff."

She didn't intend to push him completely. She did plan to drive him further to the brink. But when she leaned forward to kiss him, he guided her hips and pressed her down against his groin, reclaiming the control she would gladly relinquish at the moment. Leaning back, he used his one good hand to work his T-shirt over his head and tossed it aside, giving her an up close view of the stellar chest that had held a large group of women captive earlier that evening. A panorama of muscle and taut skin and a thin stream of hair that disappeared into his jeans. Talk about happy trails.

"Your turn," he said. "Unless you're too shy."

She'd never considered herself to be that reserved, but she couldn't claim she wasn't a tad self-conscious. She also couldn't resist a good challenge.

With that in mind, she began unbuttoning the blouse, slowly, keeping her gaze trained on his eyes. Two more buttons and a bra stood between her and flesh-to-flesh contact.

She paused before releasing the placket completely. Was this really happening? Was she seriously about to finally end her self-imposed celibacy with one of the sexiest men in the country? Heck yeah, she was…

As long as the person rapping on the door would go away.

"Ignore it," Houston grumbled.

Jill made an effort to do that very thing, honestly she did, but the knocking didn't stop. In fact, it only grew louder.

When she climbed off Houston's lap and began redoing the blouse, Houston groaned. As an after-thought, she grabbed a throw pillow from the club chair and tossed it at him. "You might want to cover your current predicament, in case my mother's on the threshold."

"Or I could just wait for you in the bedroom."

"Stay put. I'll get rid of her fast."

"And I'd buy tickets to that."

After a brief mental pep talk, she opened the door, not to her mother, but to her sister still wearing her pink cocktail dress and matching heels. And before Jill could utter a word, Pamela brushed past her and entered the pool house like a Texas Tornado. A regular chip off the old storm.

Pamela spun around and faced Jill, her back to the sofa where Houston still sat, shirtless, apparently unnoticed by the flustered sister. "I thought I'd find you here," she said. "You should have left me a note."

Since when did she have to answer to her sibling? She didn't bother to close the door in hopes that Pamela would take the hint. "If you're here to scold me, consider me scolded. I'm sure you're anxious to get to bed and get some rest before the big day, so have a great night."

"Actually, I came here to tell you I covered for you with Mother."

"Did she do a bed check?"

"No. She sent me upstairs to tell you she had something to discuss with you. When I found you gone, I told her you had a headache and you'd talk to her tomorrow."

"And I'm sure she asked if I was alone."

"Of course."

"Well, thanks, Pamela. Sleep well."

"That's not all."

Great. "All right. What else?"

"Are you going to be here all night?"

"That's the plan."

"Good, because I need the room all to myself."

Her sister's selfishness never ceased to amaze her. "I promise I will not grace your inner sanctum until tomorrow morning so that you have privacy to prepare for the nuptials."

"I need my privacy because Clark's here." Pamela moved to the still-open door and said, "It's okay. You can come in."

Lovely. A prewedding party in the pool house. Jill didn't recall sending out any invitations.

Clark stepped inside, hands in pockets, looking a little uncomfortable. "Hey, folks."

"Hey, Clark," Houston said from the sofa, his first

words since the disruption. Fortunately he'd put on his shirt. "Anyone else out there in the yard?"

Clark grinned. "Not unless the hurricane saw me drive in."

"Hi, Houston," Pam said before she punched Clark's arm. "I told you to turn off the headlights."

He caught her hand and continued to hold it, either out of affection or self-preservation. "I did, but your mother has a built-in radar."

Jill simply wanted everyone to vacate the premises so she and Houston could continue their alone time. "Well, it's good to see you both, and rest assured I won't say a word about your sneaking the groom into your bedroom for some prehoneymoon playtime."

"Good, because you owe me one," Pam said.

"Excuse me?"

"Remember that time you and Millie sneaked out at midnight to go to Billy Haverkamp's house for a party?"

She did, though she'd prefer to forget it. "Yes. And your point?"

"I never told a soul about it, even the part where you came home drunk and threw up."

Jill ignored Houston's chuckling. "And I thanked you profusely before I found out you told Clark and he told his mother and his mother told ours."

"Sorry about that," Clark muttered. "I didn't know you were both going to be grounded almost the entire summer."

That fateful summer when she'd lost her best

friend. Jill glanced at the clock hanging above the kitchenette. "If we're finished with the trip down memory lane, it's almost eleven o'clock, which means you only have an hour before you'll have to go your separate ways."

Pam looked perplexed. "Why?"

"It's bad luck for me to see the bride on the day of the wedding." Clark brought his attention to Jill. "Before we go, I need some advice."

"You might want to talk to me about that," Houston said.

Clark smiled as he wrapped his arm around Pamela. "It's about the wedding. We have a chair reserved in memory of Millie. Pam thinks we should put flowers there, but I believe it should be more personal. Do you have any ideas?"

Jill's emotions began to rise, putting a definite damper on the evening. Yet she did have a good suggestion that would do the memorial justice. "Do you still have her championship ribbons?"

Clark glanced at Pamela. "Yes. They're still hanging on a bulletin board in her room. Everything is still there. Mom didn't have the heart to change it."

Jill's heart did a nosedive. "Then I'd use those ribbons. They meant so much to Millie."

Clark surprisingly drew her into a hug. "Thanks, soon-to-be sister-in-law."

Clearly she had misjudged him. The jury was still out on her sister. "You're welcome. I know you miss her as much as I do."

Pamela sighed. "I miss her, too." She gave Jill a

meaningful look. "I miss the you before Millie died. The you who used to help me with my homework and took me to riding lessons and watched movies with me. You changed so much after you lost Millie that I barely remember my big sister."

The truth in Pamela's words stung like a scorpion. "I didn't realize how much that affected you."

"It did," Pamela said. "But I just want that sister back now."

This time Jill made the first move and drew her into an embrace. "I'm sorry, Pam. We'll start over."

Pam moved back and sniffed. "We better. If we'd done this sooner, I wouldn't have had to ask Cousin Tisha to be in the wedding. I would have asked you instead. But most important, I want to spend time with my niece or nephew."

Jill started to set her straight on the pregnancy misunderstanding but decided to save it for another conversation, after the wedding. "I promise to stay in touch."

"We'll hold you to it," Clark said. "Right now we're going to leave you two alone to go back to doing whatever you were doing before we interrupted."

With the sudden change in the mood, Jill hoped that was possible.

After Clark and Pam said their goodbyes and left, she turned to Houston, who was standing next to the sofa. "That was interesting, to say the least."

"I'd say it was pretty enlightening. Come here."

Jill walked easily into his outstretched arms and

they stood there for a time, her head on his strong shoulder, holding each other. Houston seemed to know what she needed, and she found that to be a wonderful and welcome surprise.

After a brief span of silence, Jill pulled back and stared into his eyes. "What now?"

"That's up to you. If you want to go to bed to get some sleep, I'm okay with that."

"I'm not," Jill blurted out. "I need to be with you."

"I need that, too, but only if you're really ready."

She did need the closeness, the intimacy. She needed him much more than she should. "I trust you can make me very ready."

His grin arrived, slow as warm maple syrup, and just as sweet. "Darlin', you can count on that."

Without warning, he swooped her up into his arms, causing Jill to panic. "You're going to injure your wrist again, Houston."

"Not if I'm careful, which I am." He nudged the bedroom door open. "You'll figure that out real soon."

After he deposited her onto the bed, he whipped off his T-shirt and his hand came to rest on the button securing his fly. "You still have time to back out."

She leaned back and supported her weight on bent elbows. "Never. Continue."

Jill held her breath as Houston lowered his zipper, and released it slowly when he shoved down his jeans and boxers. *Oh, wow. Oh, my.* He was extremely happy to see her.

After removing his pants completely, he threw

them onto the adjacent bed and smiled. "Your turn. I'd help you, but with this bum hand, it'd take me all night just getting those buttons undone."

Now or never had arrived. She chose now. With one exception. "Okay, as soon as you shut off the light."

"No way."

"Yes, way."

"But I want to see you."

"There's enough light coming in through the window. I just don't want to feel like I'm in the spotlight the first time." Which sounded as if she planned to have a second time. Stranger things had happened, namely finding herself in a bedroom at her parents' home with a naked Houston Calloway. Who would've thought that? Not her.

Houston trudged back to the door and flipped the switch, but not before he gave her a good look at his remarkable butt. Good times.

With the room now washed in the slight glow from the guard light outside the window, Houston took a seat next to his discarded jeans and waited for the official undressing.

Jill scooted off the bed and stood on shaky legs. Her hands also shook when she unbuttoned the blouse, but she managed to get it off. She had little trouble removing her shorts. She sensed Houston's gaze as she reached behind her, unhooked the bra and slid it off. Only one barrier remained, and with only a mild hesitation, she hooked her thumbs in the lacy band and let the thong slide down her legs.

After she kicked off her panties, she remained frozen on the spot, wondering and waiting for what would come next.

What seemed an interminable amount of time passed before Houston rose and took her hand. He then led her back to the too-small twin, threw back the covers and positioned them on the bed where they somehow managed to find enough space to lie side by side. "You're incredible," he said and then brushed his lips across her temple. "Incredible mind." He kissed her cheek. "Incredible conviction." He lowered his mouth to her throat. "Damn incredible body."

When he drew her breast into his mouth, Jill involuntarily lifted her hips from the sensations. She felt as if every nerve she owned came alive when he circled his tongue around her nipple, softly, slowly. After he paid equal attention to her other breast, he rose above her and kissed her with such tenderness. "It's not too late to stop, Jill."

She didn't care to stop. Ever. "I promise I'm still ready."

"Not quite, but you will be." He slid his hand slowly down her belly and kept going until he reached the apex of her thighs.

He used his fingertip like a feather, stroking her lightly, then more deliberately, until Jill felt as if she couldn't stay still. She closed her eyes, immersed in sensations much stronger than they had been in the limo. The orgasm hit her swift and sure and much,

much too soon, yet Houston didn't let up until all her spasms subsided.

"You're plenty ready now," he whispered. "If you're sure you want to go through with this."

She'd never wanted anything more in her life. "I'm sure," she managed through her uneven breathing.

"Okay."

Houston left the bed and began to rifle through a bag on the floor. He came back and perched on the edge of the mattress. Jill heard what she gathered was the opening of a plastic packet and realized condom time had come. That led to a burning question. "Did you bring those along just in case?"

"I never assumed anything," he said. "But I'm always prepared."

Of course he would be. After all, she wasn't his first conquest. Probably not by a long shot.

Jill refused to let that hinder the prospect of being with him in every way. Of finally feeling like a normal, healthy, sexual being, though she recognized this first foray into lovemaking wouldn't be comfortable.

"I'm going to try not to hurt you too much, sweetheart," Houston said as he rolled the condom into place. "Just hold tight to me."

Exactly what she planned to do when he shifted on top of her. She gritted her teeth when he eased inside her, and clasped the sheet in her fist when he met her body's initial resistance. After a short thrust, he drew in a deep breath and stilled, giving her time to adjust to the pressure before he began to move easily, gently. "Damn, you feel good," he said in a harsh tone. "Too good to last long."

Jill could tell he was holding back, and she truly didn't want that. "I'm okay," she told him. "It's okay for you to let go. I can handle it."

Her words seemed to unearth something in Houston, a little bit of wildness and a whole lot of strength. She moved with him, the pain all but forgotten, as she ran her palms down the solid plane of his back and the pearls of his spine.

She kept going to his hips, relishing the play of his muscles until he tensed from his own climax. He muttered a few sexy oaths that would send Hurricane Helen into a tailspin, yet they enthralled Jill. When he rolled onto his back, he hit some part of his right arm on the wall and muttered a few more.

Houston then slid his arm beneath her shoulders and asked, "Are you okay, darlin'?"

"I should be asking if you're okay. Please tell me you didn't fracture your good arm."

"I'm fine. I just hit my funny bone, but it wasn't a damn bit funny."

"You actually tweaked your ulnar nerve, not a bone. It'll go away soon."

"Man, I just love medical pillow talk."

Jill couldn't help but laugh. "Sorry. Don't forget I'm a rookie."

He nuzzled her neck. "But you act like a pro."

"Yeah, right. I still have a lot to learn."

"I'm a good teacher."

Jill's defenses went on high alert. "I doubt we have enough time left this weekend for too many lessons."

"We still have tomorrow night."

Time to reveal what she'd decided earlier today. "Since the wedding's at four, if it's okay with you, I'd like to fly back to Texas tomorrow evening. That way I'll have all day Sunday to relax before I dive into work on Monday."

He remained quiet for a few moments before he spoke again. "Sure, if that's what you want. But I figure your family's going to be disappointed by your early departure."

"My dad, maybe, but not my mother."

"You need to work things out with her, Jill."

Where had that come from? "That's a lost cause, Houston."

"Only if you give up. Life is short and parents don't live forever. Believe me, you don't want things left unsaid, unless you don't mind dealing with a truckload of regrets."

Jill surmised he was speaking from personal experience. "Does this have to do with your father?"

"Yeah."

"Do you want to talk about it?"

"If I do, then you'll never see me in the same way again."

"Why don't you let me be the judge of that?"

He stayed silent for a few seconds, then sighed. "It's one helluva sorry story, and a damn heavy secret, but maybe it's time for me to tell someone. So here goes…"

Ten

He didn't know why he felt the need to tell her. He didn't know where to begin. In reality he did know—the day he'd dishonored his dad.

Houston scooted up against the headboard and waited a minute to corral his thoughts before he spoke. "My father called me one night and told me he was under the weather. He asked me to cancel my next event and come home to help out with the ranch. I told him that would mess up my points and I might not make it to the finals. I figured that would be the end of it."

"But it wasn't," Jill said from her place beside him.

"Not by a long shot. He told me I had my priorities screwed up, like he had any right to lecture me on priorities after what he did to my mom and Jen, although I didn't know about that at the time. Anyway, it's what I said to him before I hung up that's been eating away at me for seven years."

When he paused to take a breath, Jill touched his arm. "You don't have to continue tonight."

If he didn't, he might just keep it bottled up for the next thirty-one years. "No, I want to tell you everything."

She sat up and tipped her head against his shoulder. "I'm listening."

He hesitated a second before continuing. "He started lecturing me about responsibilities and how I needed to grow up and be a man, not a boy. Then he said, 'I love you, son, but I'm not getting any younger. I don't know how much time I have left.'" A direct quote that had been branded in his brain. "I was so pissed off I told him that with my luck, he'd live forever. He passed away two days later."

"Oh, Houston, I'm so sorry."

He sighed. "So am I. Sorry I said it. Sorry I can't take it back. No matter how many flaws he had, or that he spent a lot of time away from home, when we thought he was away on business, I still loved him. He taught all of us how to rope and ride and tend cattle. He came to our rodeos when he had time. He was stern, but fair, and he told us he was proud more times than I can count."

"I guess his downfall would have to be falling in love with two women."

"Three if you count Dallas and Austin's mom." He let go a cynical laugh. "I've never fallen in love with one woman." Until now.

The thought sent alarm bells sounding in Houston's mind. He might care for Jill, but love? Nah. He chalked up the foreign feelings to sex with a woman who'd never been with another man. A great woman who'd trusted him enough to give him what his mother would say was the ultimate gift.

He scooted back down in the bed, taking Jill with him. When he slid his arms beneath her shoulders, she shifted to her side and laid her head on his chest. "I hope you don't think any less of me," he said after a time.

"Of course not. You made a mistake and said things you didn't mean. I'm sure your father knew that."

If only he could believe that. "I did learn something. Life is damn short. It's always good to forgive your parents' sins and let them know you love them before it's too late."

Jill's silence told Houston she was taking the advice in. "You're right," she said. "Before I leave tomorrow, I'm going to try to mend my relationship with my mother."

"And tell her the truth about us?"

"Yes, though I'm not sure if she'll be relieved we're not a couple, or angry because I lied about it."

"Friends who enjoyed some mighty fine benefits."

"Oh, yeah. Mighty fine."

He kissed the top of her head. "I guess you'll just have to hope for the best, and prepare for Hurricane Helen to blow."

"Jillian Elizabeth Amherst, what do you mean you made all this up?"

Jill surveyed the area around the tent to see who had heard her mother's outburst. Fortunately the post-wedding champagne was flowing and everyone in attendance seemed more interested in that instead of their conversation. "I thought you'd be glad to know you're not going to be a grandmother."

Helen sent a quick glance at Houston, who stood off to the side a few yards away chatting up her husband, both out of the hurricane's immediate path. "And you're not engaged to him?"

"No. We're friends and colleagues. I'll be working on the ranch as their resident athletic trainer for a camp geared to aspiring cowboys."

"Yet you shacked up with him in the pool house all night."

So much for her sister covering for her. "What difference does it make? We're both adults."

"Clearly consenting adults, and there is no telling what you consented to."

Jill made an effort not to look too guilty. "I'm an adult, Mother. I don't need a nanny any longer."

"It appears you need a keeper, Jillian. Why did you lie to me in the first place?"

"Because I didn't want to come here and face a slew of prospective boyfriends lined up by you and your friends. Instead, I brought my own pretend beau."

"That is ridiculous. I've never lined up boyfriends for you."

"Never, Mother?"

Helen glanced away. "Perhaps once or twice. You rarely came home after you left for college."

She should have predicted that dig. So much for the healing process. "Anyway, I basically wanted to set the record straight and tell you we're about to fly back to Texas."

"Tonight?"

"Yes. I need to be back to prepare for work on Monday."

"You're going to miss the cake cutting and the bouquet tossing, not to mention the fireworks."

She'd witnessed enough fireworks for one weekend. "I'm sure I'll see all the photos."

"Are you going to say goodbye to your sister?"

"I already have." And they'd even hugged a lot and cried a little when they'd gathered by Millie's memorial chair covered in her riding ribbons and white roses.

"She made a beautiful bride and she's chosen a great groom."

Helen eyed her suspiciously. "You've never cared for Clark."

"You're right, back when he was Millie's bratty little brother. But he's changed for the better."

Helen wrung her hands and fretted for a few moments. "Well, have a good flight, although I hate the thought of your traveling in coach."

Boy, this was going to be fun. "I'm traveling in Houston's private plane."

Her mother's eyes went as wide as a balloon. "He makes that much money? He must be a very good male model."

At least that was better than the porn star assumption. "He's not a male model. He's a world champion bull rider and spokesperson for several sponsors. He's also a partner in an extremely successful ranching operation."

"Then he's rich?"

The enthusiasm in her mother's query was unmistakable. "You could say that."

"Why didn't you say so sooner? I would have welcomed him into our home with open arms."

Typical Helen. "Mother, I hope someday you'll realize it's not the size of a man's wallet that matters, it's the wealth in his soul. If Houston didn't have a penny to his name, he still has an abundance of honor. The woman who lands him is going to be one lucky girl."

Helen stared at her straight on. "You wish you were that woman."

The comment stunned Jill into momentary silence. "I never said that."

"You don't have to. I can see it in your eyes and hear it in your voice. You're falling in love with him, if you haven't already."

She couldn't quite wrap her mind around her mother's theory. "As I've said, we're only friends."

Helen hooked her arm through Jill's and led her farther away from Houston before facing her again. "I know his kind, Jill. He's a very handsome and charming young man, just like your father was at that age. Of course, Benjamin wasn't quite as rugged. Nevertheless, if you're not careful, you could find yourself in the same predicament I was at your age. Actually I was much younger then."

"What predicament?"

"Pregnant out of wedlock."

If the grassy lawn opened up and consumed her, Jill couldn't be more shocked. "I thought you and Daddy were married ten months before I was born."

"That's what we told everyone to save face. In truth, we eloped a month after I found out I was expecting you."

Now her mother's attitude had begun to make perfect sense. "And that's why you scared the bejeezus out of me when it came to premarital sex. I thought you had an aversion to it."

Helen shook her head. "Not in the least. Why, even now, your father and I—"

"Let's not go there, Mother."

"All right."

Jill did have a serious question that needed to be asked. "Is that also why you resented me for most of my life?"

Helen looked sincerely taken aback. "I've never resented you, Jillian. I might have been ill-prepared to be a mother at twenty-two, but the moment I held you that first time, I knew that I could never love another soul as much as I loved you, aside from your father and your sister."

More stunning revelations. "It always seemed Pamela was your favorite."

Helen waved a hand, her trademark dismissive gesture. "Oh, pooh. Pamela was an easier child. You were more challenging. You climbed trees in your Sunday best and argued at the drop of a hat. But I've always loved you, even when you've disappointed me."

Well, she couldn't expect her mother's attitude to change overnight, but at least this verbal exchange was a start to understanding her motives. "You're referring to my career choice."

"Yes, I suppose I am, but you're obviously successful at it, although I don't fully understand how you get any satisfaction out of treating injuries. I'm proud of you and I still love you as much as I did on the first day we met."

The words that Jill had longed to hear for years. "Thank you, Mother, and I love you, too, even when I don't understand your need to judge people, and when you've harassed me about copulation."

Helen frowned. "I may not be perfect, Jillian, but I will always be your mother."

"Yes, and we still have a long way to go to mend our relationship."

"I'm willing if you are."

She was, too, more willing than she'd ever been. "I am, but right now I have to go back to work."

They shared a somewhat awkward hug before walking side by side as they approached Houston. "You take care with my daughter, Mr. Calloway. And if you're going to be associated with this family, I'd prefer that you don't pose half-naked again. It's going to take months to explain why my daughter's fiancé, *presumed* fiancé, would do such a thing."

Typical Helen, Jill thought, yet Houston responded with a winning grin. "You bet, Mrs. Amherst."

"Please, you may call me Helen," she said. "As long as you don't precede it with *Hurricane.*"

"It's a deal, Helen without the hurricane." He regarded Jill then. "Winston put the bags in the car and the plane's ready when you are."

"I'm ready."

After giving her mother another fast hug and her dad a lengthy embrace, she crossed the lawn with Houston, walked back through the house and entered the Bentley for the ride to the airport.

"How'd that conversation with your mom go?" Houston asked after they'd settled into the sedan.

"Better than expected," she answered. "I did learn an interesting tidbit."

"She doesn't despise me any longer now that she knows I didn't put a bun in your oven?"

"Yes, and she's thrilled to learn you have a bank account, but that's not what I was referring to. I found out my father put a bun in her oven before they married. That bun is me."

Houston laughed. "Old Ben. Didn't know he had it in him."

"Apparently he did and still does, although I halted that topic with my mother before she scarred me for life. All in all, it went fairly well, although realistically we still have miles before we get back on track. She even told me she loved me for the first time in a long time."

Houston went strangely silent. "Did you say it back?"

After their conversation last night, she knew exactly why that seemed so important to him. "Yes, I did, and I told my sister and my father and even Clark, so all is right with the Amherst family for the time being."

He slid her hand into his and gave it a little squeeze, yet he failed to look at her. "I'm real glad for you, Jill."

They stayed that way until they reached the airport, holding hands and immersed in comfortable quiet. But Houston's continued silence during and after takeoff bothered Jill a bit.

"What's on your mind, Calloway?" she asked after she grabbed a soda from the fridge and reclaimed her seat.

"Nothing much. I was just thinking I kind of hate that the weekend's coming to an end."

"Technically not until tomorrow."

He locked his gaze on hers. "I meant our weekend together. I've had a damn good time."

She smiled. "So did I. That was one unforget-table night."

"In a good way, I hope."

"A very good way."

"Are you feeling any ill effects?"

"I was a little uncomfortable this morning, but I'm fine now."

His devilish grin came out of hiding. "It's always better the second time around."

He'd gone from sullen to sexy in five seconds flat. "Are you trying to compromise me, Calloway?"

"That depends, Amherst. Do you want to be com-promised?"

She decided to leave him in suspense. "I'll let you know when we land."

"I don't want to wait to compromise you. We've got three hours to kill, a bed in the back and no one around."

Jill resisted the urge to climb out of the chair and tackle him. "Sounds interesting."

"Interesting enough to take me up on the offer?"

She didn't have to think twice. "I could use some benefits to go along with our friendship." A friend-ship that had taken a remarkable turn.

"You've come to the right cowboy for that."

How well she knew that.

Houston pulled her to her feet and led her into the back of the plane, where he opened a sliding door to compact sleeping quarters. The double bed, covered in navy and beige, practically took up the entire space with very little room on the sides. Obviously Houston was more than aware of that issue, Jill realized, when he sat her down on the end of the mattress.

"I like this dress," he said as he unhooked the back of the collar, allowing the blue halter bodice to fall to her waist. "No bra, huh? I really like it now."

Jill liked the way he made her feel when he finessed her breasts with his talented mouth. She liked the way he streamed his hands up her thighs. She seriously liked the sensual words he whispered in her ears as he reached beneath her skirt and slid her panties away.

And when he went to his knees and feathered kisses on the inside of her thighs, she grew excited with anticipation, and became slightly nervous. "Where are you going, Calloway?"

He lifted his head and grinned. "Where I assume no man has gone before."

"You would be correct."

His smile dropped out of sight, replaced by a concerned expression. "Do you trust me?"

"Yes, I do." And she did…enough to let him continue.

"Are you sure?"

"Very."

"Good. Now just relax and enjoy it."

Enjoy it, yes. Relax, no way. Not when he worked the dress up, parted her legs and his mouth hit the mark. This ultimate intimacy drove all thoughts from her mind. She tuned in to every nuance, every sensation until her body's natural course took over.

The orgasm hit swift and sure and didn't last long enough for Jill.

As if Houston agreed, he didn't let up with the soft, steady strokes of his tongue and amazingly drew out another climax, leaving her trembling and struggling for breath. Wrestling with the fact she'd never felt this way before.

Jill fell back on the bed and closed her eyes, absolutely amazed that she had done that twice. Correction. Houston had helped her do it twice. She shouldn't be so surprised. Everything he endeavored to do, he did it well.

She opened her eyes to see him standing at the bed, shirtless, removing his jeans. She shimmied out of her dress and when they were both naked, he joined her on the bed, condom in hand.

He rolled to face her and smiled. "How do you feel?"

She touched his shadowed jaw. "Like I just had a double scoop of chocolate chip ice cream while on a cruise to the Caribbean."

"That good, huh?"

"That good."

"Are you ready to keep cruising?"

"I sure am." Feeling bold, she snatched the packet from his grip, tore it open and removed the condom. "FYI, this is also a first for me, so be patient."

He looked somewhat wary. "No offense, but this isn't a good time to practice. If you put even a little nick in it—"

"Look, Houston, I put on gloves all the time without any issues. I can handle this."

"Yeah, but—"

"Do you trust me?" she asked as she nudged him onto his back and ran a fingertip down the length of him.

He groaned. "I guess I don't have any choice if you keep doing that."

"Then just stop worrying and enjoy."

She did a bit more playing and he did a bit more groaning before she finally had the condom in place, although it hadn't been quite as easy as she'd presumed it would be. Now that she appeared to be in control for a change, she straddled his legs and guided him inside her.

"You're just full of surprises, aren't you, darlin'?"

"Yes, I am," she said proudly. "And just because I'm a novice doesn't mean I'm not a quick learner."

She demonstrated that by moving slowly, all the while watching the change in his eyes and expression. Drunk on the power of seduction, she moved faster and noticed his respiration increasing.

Seeing the moment he reached his own climax was a true wonder to behold. Knowing she'd been responsible for it made her want to strut around the plane. Instead, she rested her cheek against his chest and listened to his heartbeat return to normal.

Jill stayed that way for a time before shifting onto her back beside him. "You are in so much trouble," she said in a teasing tone.

"Why is that?"

"I'm starting to really like this."

He released a low laugh. "I've created a sex monster?"

"I wouldn't go that far, but I realize now what I've been missing." Making love with a skilled, careful man.

He rolled her into his arms, held her tightly. "If someone had told me a month ago that I'd have you in my bed, I would've said they were crazy."

Her heart sank. "I didn't know I repulsed you that much."

He pressed a kiss on her forehead. "Exactly the opposite. I used to find excuses to see you when I was on the circuit."

"Come on, Houston. You weren't injured that often."

"True, so didn't you think it was kind of strange when I used to show up in the tent with my friends and fellow bull riders and I didn't have a scratch on me?"

In hindsight, he had. Often. "I assumed you wanted to give me a hard time."

"I assumed that, too, but I didn't want to admit to myself, or anyone else, that I was damn attracted to you."

"You had a weird way of showing that."

"Not anymore." He topped off the comment with a light kiss between her breasts, putting her senses once more on high alert.

She rose above him and kissed his chin. "We still

have a good two hours left, so did you bring any more of those condoms?"

"Unfortunately, no. But I've got plenty at my house, and a king-size bed. We could actually have some space for a change, although we don't really need much."

Jill needed to keep her head on straight. "That would break our rule about no fooling around on the ranch."

He touched her face gently. "Stay with me just one more night."

Logic told her to say no, but her illogical heart urged her to shout yes. "Okay. One more night. But after that, we go back to the way it was before this weekend. You harass me—I scold you."

His smile arrived, but only halfway. "If that's the way you want it, then that's the way it will be."

The disappointment in his tone surprised Jill. Did he want something more? A real relationship with potential for a future?

Wishful thinking, of course. Houston Calloway was a risk chaser who wouldn't welcome anything permanent at this point in time. In a matter of weeks, he would be gone again, immersed in the thrill of the rodeo, and all she would have would be the memories of a wonderful, wild weekend with a charming cowboy.

After he climbed off the mechanical bull, Houston realized he hadn't felt this satisfied since…well…last night with Jill in his bed. The vow they'd made to return to only friendship had gone up in smoke several times since they'd gotten back to the ranch. He chalked it up to uncontrolled lust, and he figured that need for each other would probably run its course.

But not soon, he decided, when he saw Jill standing in the opening of the enclosed training arena, her silky auburn hair piled atop her pretty head in a sexy ponytail. She wore a blue-and-white plaid shirt rolled up at the sleeves, a pair of great-fitting jeans and the brown boots he'd bought her two days ago as a surprise. She also sported a look that said she didn't exactly appreciate finding him on a moving animal, even if it happened to be a bad imitation of the real thing.

Houston strode toward Jill, intent on kissing that sour look off her face, regardless of the ranch hands milling around the area. He nixed that plan when she folded her arms across her middle and glared.

"Did you have fun with that?" she asked, not even bothering to hide her anger.

He shrugged. "Not really. The damn thing was going so slow even Chance could have ridden it."

"And that would have been wonderful with his cracked collarbone."

Damn, he couldn't win for losing. "Do you want to try it?"

"No, I do not."

She spun around and headed toward the clinic at a quick clip, keeping her back to him.

After he caught up to her, Houston clasped her

arm and turned her around. "Don't get your feathers ruffled, Jill. I was just testing it out. No harm done."

"Maybe not now, but what about later, when you get back on a real bull?"

"I'm still a few weeks away from that."

"If you don't permanently injure yourself before then."

"I'm being careful."

"All signs point to the opposite."

He sensed something else might be behind her irritability. "What's really going on here, Jill?"

"Nothing, aside from the fact that I worry about you."

He winked. "Aw, darlin', what a sweet thing to say."

She rolled her eyes. "Of course I care. I don't want you damaging your wrist more than you already have. Dallas made me promise I'd keep you out of trouble."

He wrapped his good arm around her waist and reeled her in close. "You shouldn't make promises you can't keep, although last night you definitely kept one promise I'm not going to forget for a long, long time."

Jill surveyed the area and frowned again. "Hush. Do you want everyone knowing our business?"

"Who cares?"

"I do. Now unhand me, you cad, so I can get back to work."

He brushed a kiss across her mouth before handing her a suggestion he'd been thinking about all morning. "I have a better idea. You should take a ride."

"Houston, seriously, I don't have time for afternoon delight."

Man, that conjured up a lot of great fantasies. Time to return to the original plan. "I meant a ride on a horse."

Now she looked alarmed. "I told you it's been too long."

"Yep, you're right. Way too long, and that's why you just need to do it."

Before Jill could protest further, Houston took her hand and led her toward the barn. She stayed silent while he led Gabby out of the stall and began to tack up the mare. "You'll have to ride Western," he said and he set the saddle on her back. "Hope that works."

"I haven't agreed to ride yet."

He fitted the bit in Gabby's mouth and adjusted the headstall. "You're dying to do it, so don't even bother arguing."

"You think you know me so well."

Better than he ever believed he would know her. "I know you need to prove to yourself that you can do it."

He turned to find her staring off into space. "I don't need to prove anything."

Time to bring out the big guns, in spite of the risk. "If Millie were here, what would she say to you?"

Her gaze snapped to his. "That's not fair."

Probably not, and he didn't want to cause her pain.

He just wanted to move her into the present and out of the past. "Answer the question, Jill."

Her expression turned from anger to resignation. "She'd call me a wimp and tell me get on the damn horse."

Houston realized that might be the first time he'd heard a curse word coming out of her mouth. "Good advice. Just a couple of turns in the round pen. If you're not comfortable, you can get off and call it a day."

"Okay," she said as she took the reins from him. "But only for a few minutes."

Houston trailed behind Jill as she led the mare out of the barn and into the nearby pen. She stopped in the center of the circle to tighten the girth strap and adjust the stirrups, then hesitated with her hand on the saddle horn.

"Need some help climbing on?" Houston asked from his position near the gate.

She sent him a frustrated look over one shoulder. "No, I don't."

Jill mounted the horse with ease, proving her point, then cued Gabby into a walk. She made two rounds and Houston figured that would be it. Then she surprised him when she began to trot, bouncing up and down in the seat like a practiced English rider. He couldn't deny his surprise over how at home she looked on a horse. He also couldn't ignore the pleasure in her face as she kept going.

After a time, Houston decided a little encouragement was in order. "You should try a lope."

"No," she said. "But I will try a canter."

No sooner than she'd said it, she did it, as easy as you please.

Houston stood there and watched with pride as she rounded the ring again and again. He couldn't believe she'd agreed to this. He couldn't believe how thrilled she looked. He really couldn't understand why her happiness seemed to matter so much to him, but it did. *She* mattered to him, more than he cared to admit.

Maybe he just liked the fact she'd overcome some fairly sorry memories from her past. Maybe he wished at some point in time he could do the same, but that didn't seem all that likely.

A few minutes later, Jill dismounted and guided Gabby toward Houston, a bright smile on her face. "That was great."

So was the excitement Houston saw in her green eyes. "You're a natural, Jill."

She patted the mare's neck. "She's a natural. I'm just a passenger."

"Don't think for a minute she believes that. Neither do I."

She gave him a meaningful look. "Thank you, Houston. I'm not sure I would have ever gotten back on a horse if not for you."

He considered that one high compliment. "I didn't do anything aside from providing a vehicle. And you can ride her all you want while I'm gone."

Her frown reappeared. "Where are you going?"

Somewhere he didn't care to go, but business

called. "I have to head out tomorrow to Los Angeles for a photo shoot."

"With your clothes on, I hope."

"I don't fly naked unless you're with me."

She laughed. "I meant naked photos."

"Nope. I'll be fully clothed in cowboy garb."

"Good to know. Now I need to get her unsaddled and get back to work."

He grabbed the reins from her and realized he didn't want to leave her now, or at all, truth be known. But he had no choice. He did have one thing he could control, if she was willing. "I'll take care of Gabby, on one condition."

"You and your conditions. What now?"

"Stay with me tonight, sweetheart. Your place, my place, it doesn't matter. I'm going to be gone for a while, and I'd like a good send-off."

For a second she looked torn before she smiled again. "All right, I suppose." She pointed at him. "But this has to be the last time, Houston, otherwise someone will find out, namely Dallas, and I'll lose my job."

He refused to let his brother interfere in his personal life. "Don't worry about Dallas. I can handle him." He brushed a wayward lock of hair away from her cheek. "Let's just concentrate on having one last wild night and making some mighty fine memories."

Jill stared at the reminder of her continued careless behavior for a good five minutes. She'd taken a huge chance on being carefree, and now she would pay for it. Maybe she'd been attacked by the cruel hand of karma, a self-fulfilling prophecy for allowing her family to believe she was pregnant. And now she was.

When the doorbell sounded, she immediately tossed the plastic stick into the bathroom's trash bin in a blind panic, ill-prepared to face the father of her unborn child.

She drew in a deep breath and attempted to calm down. After all, Houston had been gone for the past week, and she didn't expect him to return for another two days. But what if he'd cut the trip short?

If that happened to be the case, she didn't have to say anything yet, not until she figured out exactly what she would say.

When the bell sounded again, Jill walked slowly to the entry and peeked through the peephole. Her shoulders sagged with relief when she discovered Georgie, not Houston, standing on the porch.

She tried on a casual expression and opened the door. "Hey there. What a great surprise."

Georgie looked confused. "You asked me to stop by for coffee at nine. And it's two minutes after."

Darn if she hadn't done that very thing. "I'm so sorry. I've been distracted lately with all the staff issues and stocking supplies." And baby surprises.

"No problem. We can postpone until tomorrow."

Jill gestured her inside. "No way. I need some company." Badly. "Come in."

"Gladly," Georgie said. "I could use some girl talk."

That, Jill could absolutely provide, if she decided to reveal what she'd learned only minutes before. But wasn't that why she'd invited Georgie over in the first place, when she'd only suspected the pregnancy? She seriously needed some counsel from a woman who would know exactly how she felt at the moment.

After Georgie entered the apartment, Jill showed her to the kitchen dinette and put the coffee on to brew. "I hope you don't mind decaf."

"Decaf's fine. I've already had two cups of the real stuff, and no sugar, just cream."

Jill poured them each a cup, set the mugs on the table and took the seat across from Georgie. She decided to begin with small talk. "How are the boys?"

"Austin's great and Chance is growing like a weed. But you would know that since you had dinner with us last night, so what's really up with you?"

Her uneasiness came out on a sigh. "It's about Houston."

Georgie's brown eyes lit up and she grinned. "I knew it! Paris and I both thought you two would hook up."

"It happened the weekend we went to Florida." And again two days later at her apartment, and once more at Houston's house, the night before he'd left for California, all details she preferred to omit.

"Austin said he saw you sneaking out of Houston's place one morning not too long ago."

So much for being discreet. "All right, we've been together a few times since, even though we swore we wouldn't do that when we came back to the ranch."

"Sometimes you don't have control over that powerful pull, Jill. It was always that way between me and Austin, even after we'd been apart six years."

"But you and Austin were in love."

"That's true, which leads me to an important question." Georgie's expression turned suddenly serious. "How do you feel about Houston?"

Good question. "Well, when I met him, I thought he was arrogant and reckless, and oh, boy, did he know exactly how to ruffle my feathers. But when we were in Florida, I saw another side to him altogether. He stepped right into the role of pretend boyfriend without missing a beat. And honestly, he's the first person who's taken on my mother, not at all an easy feat, but he did it without being snide." She looked away and smiled with remembrance. "He has this wicked sense of humor, and he's definitely a great listener. He even held me when I cried after I told him about losing my best friend years ago. I've told him things I've never told anyone."

"It sounds to me like you've completely fallen for him."

Jill's gaze snapped to Georgie. "We're becoming good friends. That's all."

Georgie sipped her coffee and sent Jill a cynical look. "Are you sure that's all?"

"I don't know." And Jill truly didn't, or maybe deep down she did. "I do know we have one huge complication hanging over us now."

"Houston's career?"

"Okay, two complications. He's determined to

keep riding bulls until he has some kind of record for championships. I'm almost positive he has no intention of settling down."

"How do you know that for sure unless you ask?"

She might be forced to ask him when she told him about the baby. Or at least if he wanted to be involved in their child's life. Somehow she knew he would, even if their relationship never amounted to more than friendship. But what if it did become more? What if Houston wanted a life partner and a family? What if he wanted her to be a permanent part of that family?

"You mentioned two complications," Georgie said, dragging Jill back into reality. "What's the second one?"

Jill prepared to blurt out the truth and deal with the possible fallout. "I'm pregnant."

Georgie's brown eyes went wide with surprise. "Oh, my gosh. When did you find out?"

"Right before you got here. I asked you to come over so you could be here for the verdict, but I couldn't wait. After what you and Austin went through, I felt like you would understand."

Georgie reached over and touched Jill's hand. "I do understand. I still remember that morning I found out I was pregnant with Chance. I also remember trying to reach Austin much later, only to learn he'd married someone else and then stupidly deciding not to tell him because I didn't want to rock the boat."

"You thought you were doing the best thing at that time."

"It was a stupid mistake. I didn't give Austin the opportunity to know his child for six years, and I've always regretted it. But that's where you and I can differ, Jill. You have no reason to wait to tell Houston."

The thought of his reaction only increased her anxiety. "I have no idea how to tell him. I mean, we used protection every time, and I can't even fathom how it happened." Although she suspected her lack of experience with condom application might be the culprit.

"It doesn't matter how," Georgie said. "It's done. Now you and Houston have to decide what to do about it."

Jill rubbed her palms over her face in an effort to erase visions of his possible reaction. "I'm afraid he's going to be furious."

"He might be mad for a time, but he'll be reasonable."

"I can't ask him to give up his career, but I can't stand the thought of him seriously injured, or worse. The prospect of losing him breaks my heart."

"That's because you're in love with him."

Jill wanted so badly to deny it, but she'd reached the point where she couldn't. "I guess you're right."

Georgie smiled. "I know I'm right."

"But how could it happen so quickly?"

"How long have you known him?"

"Two years, but—"

"And in that two years, did you ever feel excited when you saw him?"

In hindsight, she probably had, but professionalism had tamped those feelings down. "Possibly, but we spent most of that time arguing over his stubbornness."

"Let's face it. Adversity can sometimes breed passion, and you find yourself loving the very thing you thought you despised."

"I never despised Houston. I did hold him in low esteem a few times."

They engaged in a light moment with a bout of laughter before the atmosphere turned serious again. "Would you like some advice?" Georgie asked.

"I'm open to any you can give me."

"Don't wait too long to tell Houston."

"Where the hell have you been? I haven't seen you since I've been back."

When Jill spun around, Houston noticed she looked pale and tired. "Do you have to sneak up on me like that?"

"I didn't sneak up on you. I walked through the door. Now answer the question, Jill."

She eyed the cut over his eyebrow. "First, you answer a question. What happened to your head?"

He should've expected that. "A cow got caught up in the fence and I got head-butted by the heifer."

"You didn't fall off a bull?"

"Hell, no."

As predicted, she strode up to him and examined the bump. "Are you seeing double?"

He only saw the concern in her green eyes. He

only knew how much he'd missed them, and her. "It's fine, dammit. I'm fine."

Jill walked to the counter and withdrew a packet, reminding Houston of the last time they were together at the rodeo. She came back to him and dabbed at the cut. "When is this crazy risk taking going to end, Houston? When are you going to realize people care about you and don't want to see you hurt?"

As bad as he'd wanted to see her, now she'd just made him mad. "I'm a rancher, Jill. Ranchers have to take risks now and then to save the livestock. It's all a part of the life. And I can tell you right now I've dealt with cattle catastrophes hundreds of times without getting hurt. Just like I've climbed on the back of bulls hundreds of times and didn't get a scratch."

"You're too reckless, Houston, and sometimes I believe it's not going to end before you seriously injure yourself, or worse." She threw the damp antiseptic pad into the trash with a vengeance. "I guess you really don't care, do you?"

He damn sure didn't care for her attitude. "You didn't answer my question. Why have you been avoiding me?"

She crossed the room and began stacking a few boxes into a cabinet before facing him again. "As you can see, I've been very busy in here. I've started making calls to line up a contracted staff. If you want to be up and running by January, I have to get everything organized."

He wasn't buying her excuses. "It's still September. That leaves you a good three months."

"You're not counting the holidays."

"You're not being honest. Something's bugging you and I figure it has to do with me."

"Your penchant for being hardheaded is bugging me, and I'm sorry you think I've been intentionally avoiding you, but as I've said, I've been busy."

"Too busy to come to dinner with the family last night?"

"Yes."

When she looked away, Houston could tell she wasn't being completely honest. "I find that kind of strange when, to hear Dallas tell it, it's been a routine with you since I've been gone. And now that I'm back, you've suddenly broken that routine."

"Houston, I can't…"

"Can't what?"

She sighed. "I can't be around you right now. Not without risking falling back into bed with you."

Finally, the truth. She'd been all he'd thought about, too, but it wasn't solely about sex. "So what if that happened? It's damn good between us, Jill. Why don't we just see where it goes?"

"I know exactly where it would go. We'd fool around now and then, and when your cast comes off, you'll go back on the road and I'll be left here with nothing but busy work and a broken heart and something even more important."

That threw his mind off-kilter. "You can't get your heart broken if we keep it casual."

She lowered her eyes and studied the floor. "It's gone beyond that. At least it has for me."

"I'm not following you, Jill."

"Are you really that obtuse? I have feelings for you. Strong feelings, and it's not because we had sex, although that was pretty great. I see in you a strong, kind, honorable man who isn't even close to being ready to settle down."

Before he'd met her, he might have agreed. "People can change when the time is right."

"When will the time be right for you, Houston? When will you ever stop running away from your guilt over your father while chasing the high you get from riding bulls? A high that could get you killed?"

"It's who I am, Jill."

"It's what you do, not who you are. You have an opportunity here to put your talent to good use, although I'll never quite understand the lure of climbing on a raging animal and hanging on. But you could be here full-time to mentor those wannabe cowboy while spending quality time with your family."

The conversation was getting way too heavy, and making him way too uncomfortable. "I'd never ask you to give up your job."

"Normally I probably wouldn't ask you to do it, either. Under different circumstances."

"What's different about our circumstances?"

"First of all, as I've said, I really care about you. Second, we're about to take on a huge responsibility, or at least I am. Whether you'll be willing remains to be seen."

"I'm just not ready to hang around here all the time. Not when I have the chance to get one more championship next year."

"I wasn't referring to that responsibility."

"Okay. Stop talking in circles and tell me what the hell you're talking about."

"I'm talking about an error we inadvertently made. My mother's prophecy, I suppose you could say."

Her words had done little to clear up the confusion. "Prophecy?"

"If you have premarital sex, you'll get pregnant."

Oh, hell. "What are you saying, Jill?"

"I'm going to have a baby."

He felt like his head might explode. "You're telling me that you got pregnant when we used protection every damn time?" Protection that he'd worried had failed the first time, thanks to his haste. Or the second time, thanks to her inexperience.

"Yes, that's what I'm telling you."

The impact of the declaration caused him to pace around the room before he turned to her again. "You're sure it's mine?" And that had to be the stupidest question to ever leave his mouth.

Jill obviously thought so, too, he determined, when she folded her arms across her middle and glared at him. "Come to think of it, maybe it was that groomsman I accosted underneath the banquet table at the wedding. Of course it's yours, and it really hurts that you would assume otherwise."

"I'm sorry," he muttered. "I'm just so damned shocked. How long have you known?"

"I suspected it about a week ago. I confirmed it with three positive pregnancy tests."

The timeline royally pissed him off. "You should've told me the minute I came back to the ranch."

"I had to think, Houston. I had to weigh all my options before we discussed it, and I've decided I want to raise this baby, with or without you."

His anger didn't come close to going away. "I'd never abandon my child, dammit. And I sure as hell don't want you running off with it. Austin didn't know he had a son for six years and I know what it did to him when he found out he'd missed all the milestones."

"Apparently everything worked out because they seem to be very happy."

"It almost didn't happen because she didn't tell him they had a kid until years after the fact."

"But I'm not deceiving you, Houston. I'm telling you now so you can decide how you want to handle this situation."

He didn't know crap because he could barely think. "You can't just lay this on me and expect me to come up with a coherent plan."

"I don't expect that at all. Right now I want you to go away and think about being a father and what that entails. You have to decide what's more important, continuing to risk your life or raising a child."

"But I—"

"Take all the time you need, Houston, and come back to see me when we can have a logical conversation."

He planned to do that very thing, but first he had to seek out the one person who could make some sense out of this. Not one of his brothers because they would only chastise him.

"I'll talk to you later," he said as he tore out of the building to head for the main house to find his mother.

A few minutes later, he discovered her sitting in the rocker on the front porch wearing her trademark flannel shirt, jeans and braid, a glass of sweet tea in her hand. He sat in the glider across from her and sighed. "Mom, I've got one big problem."

"I can see that, *mijo*. What's troubling you?"

He surveyed the immediate area, worried they might not be alone for long. "Where's Jen?"

"In San Antonio shopping. She won't be back for hours."

"Good. I don't need an audience when I say what I have to say."

"And I need to put the pot roast in the oven soon, so just say it."

"Jill's pregnant with my baby."

He expected his mom to be furious, but she just sat there, cool as a cucumber. "Your brother is going to tan your hide, Houston."

"I don't give a damn about Dallas. I only care about what I need to do."

She leaned forward and glared at him. "You need to man up and do the right thing. You need to accept that you're going to be a papa."

"What if I suck at it?"

"You might for a while, but you'll learn to be a parent, just like every parent that has gone before you, including me. My question is, how do you feel about the baby's mother?"

"I care a helluva lot about her. Not that she doesn't piss me off now and then. But damn, she's smart. And she's beautiful, inside and out. She doesn't take any BS from me, and when I'm not with her, I miss her like crazy. But she deserves someone whose life doesn't revolve around the freaking rodeo. She deserves better than me."

Maria leaned over and touched his face. "*Mijo*, in my opinion, there is no man better for her."

"You're biased."

"Yes, but not so biased that I don't see in you a man who only wants to love and be loved. I see a man who is nothing like his papa when it comes to the way he treats women."

He managed a smile. "You taught me that."

"And I taught you well. Not that I believe you haven't slipped up a time or two and broken a few hearts along the way. But this time, you must treat Jill's heart with care. She's a good woman, and she loves you."

"Why would you think that?"

"Because while you were away, and she was with us, you were all she talked about. Dallas noticed it immediately, and so did the rest of the family. He hasn't been happy about it, but the girls are thrilled. They consider Jill a part of this family, and so should you."

Houston leaned forward and studied the porch slats. "We haven't known each other for that long."

"Some would say two years is long enough."

"I meant really known each other. I don't want to let her down."

"If you love her, you won't. But if you don't have those feelings for her, then—"

"I do love her." There, he'd said it, and the earth hadn't opened up and sucked him into some dark abyss.

"There's your answer, my sweet boy."

"I'll have to give up the rodeo, Mom."

"I know, but think of what you'll be gaining."

The thought was damn daunting. He'd have a kid, and maybe even a wife. He'd be facing two o'clock feedings and college funds. First steps and first cars and, damn, first dates. And what if he had a girl? Oh, hell.

But he'd be waking up with Jill, and going to bed with her every night. He'd be sharing both good times and bad. He'd finally have someone who really loved him. Someone he could love back without any reservations.

That alone drove him to the decision he was bound to make. Now he just had to find the right time to tell her.

Jill didn't know when she'd see Houston again. Maybe in a few days. Maybe never if he headed for the hills. But less than three hours after she'd told him about their baby, she heard a series of forceful knocks.

She'd barely opened the door before Houston rushed in, tossed his tan cowboy hat onto the end table and dropped down on the sofa. "Okay, I'm ready to talk."

Considering his stern expression, Jill couldn't exactly claim she was prepared for what he had to say. But the sooner she got this over with, the better.

On that thought, she chose to sit in the small blue club chair across from him and folded her hands in her lap. "All right. I'm ready."

He hopped off the couch like a jackrabbit, as if he had too much energy to stay seated. "First of all, I'm damn sure not ready to be a dad."

Her heart sank like an anchor. "Okay, but—"

He held up a hand to silence her. "I doubt anyone is ever really ready until they dive in, headfirst. That said, I'm going to be involved in his life. I'm going to teach him how to rope and ride and herd cattle."

"What if it's a girl?"

He mulled that over for a moment. "It's not likely given our history. Austin has a boy and so does Dallas."

"There's always a first time. Would having a daughter totally freak you out?"

"Nope. Not as long as she's just like you. Smart as hell and as pretty as a bluebonnet, although that's going to be a problem when she discovers guys in her teens."

The compliment both pleased and surprised her. His fatherly attitude thrilled her. "Thank you for the praise, and for protecting our daughter."

"Or son," he added. "And you can count on me to keep them safe. The same goes for you. I wouldn't want any harm or hurt to come to the mother of my child."

"I appreciate that, but I'm fairly good at taking care of myself."

"Dammit, Jill, would you just let me be who I am? I want to protect you. I *need* to protect you. And I want to be around you all the time."

"I'm pregnant, Houston, not fragile."

He muttered a few oaths under his breath. "I'm not talking about your current state. I'm talking about our future together."

What in the world was he getting at? "I hope that we'll endeavor to remain friends while we're raising our baby. And should you decide to marry, I would like to know you'll choose a woman who'll accept our child."

"I don't want another woman, dammit. I want you."

Okay, this was insanity. "Want me in what way?"

He strode to the chair and pulled her up right into his arms. "I want you in every way, and not just because you're having my kid."

"You mean you still want the benefits."

"Yeah, but not just the sex benefits. I want you in my bed every night and every morning. I want you with me for all the family dinners and the boring charity events. Lately I've missed you like crazy and I damn sure don't want to go through that again."

Jill took a moment to reclaim her voice. "What exactly are you saying?"

"Are you really that clueless?"

She had her suspicions, but she needed to hear it. "Pretend I am."

"I love you, dammit!" he shouted.

"Well, I love you, too!" she shouted back. "Are we crazy or what?"

Houston gave her a knee-weakening kiss before saying, "Yeah, we probably are a little bit crazy, but there's nothing wrong with that. I love you something awful, Amherst. And I believe I fell in love with you, lock, stock and barrel, a year ago when you treated my groin injury after that bull kicked me good in the cojones."

She poked him in the ribs. "I love you, too, Calloway, even if you are such a guy. And I believe I started to fall in love with you during the wedding weekend, when you let me cry on your shoulder and you stood up to my mother by inventing some unbelievable story that somehow everyone believed. I really fell in love with you the first night you made love to me with such care and consideration. I knew for certain I loved you the day you encouraged me to ride Gabby."

He winked. "I'm that good, huh?"

Very typical guy. "I'll feed your ego like a zoo animal and say yes, but only if you'll continue to make love to me that way, and often."

"Just lead the way to the bedroom, darlin'."

First, she still had one more serious aspect of the conversation they hadn't covered. "Houston, it's important you know that I don't believe we should rush into a marriage until I'm sure this is what we both want."

"Sweetheart, I'm one hundred percent sure this is what I want, and I don't see myself changing my mind ever. But if you want to wait until next month or next year, that's fine by me. Just know your mother isn't going to be happy about it."

She brushed a kiss across his cheek. "To heck with my mother. At the moment, I just want to spend a lot of time with you. We'll put the wedding on hold for now."

"By the power vested in me by the state of Texas, I now pronounce you husband and wife. You may now seal your covenant with a kiss."

Her handsome new husband, dressed in a black suit and tie, wearing his trademark matching cowboy hat, winked at Jill and smiled. "Gladly."

Following the sweetest of kisses, Jill hooked her arm through Houston's and walked down the makeshift aisle in the Calloway's historic main house. Her gaze immediately zoomed in on her mother, who was dabbing at her eyes with a handkerchief provided by Jill's dapper dad. The whole hurry-up wedding had been her suggestion, and they'd appeased her.

Hurricane Helen, one. Happy couple, big winners.

But fortunately her mother had come through during the planning of the family-only holiday wedding, even if they'd had less than two months to get it all done. Jill had selected a white satin, strapless dress with an empire waist to cover the slight baby bump even though most knew about the baby, thanks to Houston's penchant for telling everyone they knew, and a few people Jill didn't know.

As they paused by the front door, the crowd soon began to gather to ply them with good wishes, hugs and kisses, while the Calloway brothers looked on. Maria and Jen stood by the red-and-green-bedecked Christmas tree, conversing with Helen, who appeared to be a bit stunned. Jill imagined Jen had just let her in on the secret ingredients in the mint julep her mother was now clutching like a life raft.

Little Luke was crawling around on the floor at his mother's feet, as his cousin, Chance, ran through the rows of chairs. Wonderful chaos as far as Jill was concerned. In a matter of months, she and Houston would be adding to that chaos with their own baby.

Paris soon emerged from the opening to the dining room and announced, "Food is ready, so come and get it."

As the guests began to file toward the table full of treats, Houston clasped Jill's hand, halting her progress. "Not so fast," he said. "I'd like a little alone time with my bride. Actually, I'd like to start the honeymoon in a few minutes."

Jill faked a frown. "I'm eating for two, remember? And frankly I'm starving."

Houston rested his hand on her abdomen. "How is junior today?"

"She's fine."

He chuckled. "What do you think about Laredo if it's a boy?"

"Sure. And if it's a girl, we'll call her Corpus Christi, C.C. for short."

"I'll have to think on that one."

Jill didn't have to think on her decision to marry this man, even if her head still hadn't quite stopped spinning. "I seriously do love you, Calloway."

"And I seriously do love you, Amherst...wait. Am I supposed to call you Amherst-Calloway?"

"You can call me anything, honey, as long as you call me to bed and ravish me."

He nuzzled her neck and whispered, "Go grab some food fast before I take you into the coat closet and have my way with you."

She touched his face and kissed him softly. "This is going to work, isn't it?"

He narrowed his eyes. "It worked well enough to get you pregnant."

"That's not what I meant."

"I know, darlin,' and the answer to your question is yeah, it's going to work, as long as you're okay with being hitched to a cowpoke who's just a plain ol' rancher."

"I'm more than okay with that, and having my gorgeous, sexy, albeit stubborn, rancher's baby."

Only this time, they weren't pretending, about the baby or being in love, and Jillian Elizabeth Amherst wouldn't have it any other way.

* * * * *

Don't miss any of these sexy romances from
Kristi Gold!

THE RANCHER'S MARRIAGE PACT
AN HEIR FOR THE TEXAN
THE SHEIKH'S SECRET HEIR
ONE HOT DESERT NIGHT
THE SHEIKH'S SON

Available now from Harlequin Desire!

If you're on Twitter, tell us what you think of
Harlequin Desire! #harlequindesire

If you enjoyed this book, you'll love
CAN'T HARDLY BREATHE, the next book in
New York Times *bestselling author*
Gena Showalter's
ORIGINAL HEARTBREAKERS *series.*
Read on for a sneak peek!

DANIEL PORTER SAT at the edge of the bed. Again and again he dismantled and rebuilt his Glock 17. Before he removed the magazine, he racked the slide to ensure no ammunition remained in the chamber. He lifted the upper portion of the semiautomatic, detached the recoil spring as well as the barrel. Then he put everything back together.

Rinse and repeat.

Some things you had to do over and over, until every cell in your body learned to perform the task on autopilot. That way, when bullets started flying, you'd react the right way—immediately—without having to check a training manual.

When his eyelids grew heavy, he placed the gun on the nightstand and stretched out across the mattress only to toss and turn. Staying at the Strawberry Inn without a woman wasn't one of his brightest ideas. Sex kept him distracted from the many horrors that lived inside his mind. After multiple overseas military tours, constant gunfights, car bombs, finding one friend after another blown to pieces, watching his targets collapse because he'd gotten a green light and pulled the trigger…his sanity had long since packed up and moved out.

Daniel scrubbed a clammy hand over his face. In the quiet of the room, he began to notice the mental chorus in the back of his mind. Muffled screams he'd heard since his first tour of duty. He pulled at hanks of his hair, but the screams only escalated.

This. This was the reason he refused to commit to a woman. Well, one of many reasons. He was too messed up, his past too violent, his present too uncertain.

A man who looked at a TV remote as if it were a bomb about to detonate had no business inviting an innocent civilian into his crazy.

He'd even forgotten how to laugh.

No, not true. Since his return to Strawberry Valley, two people had defied the odds and amused him. His best friend slash spirit animal Jessie Kay West… and Dottie.

My name is Dorothea.

She'd been two grades behind him, had always kept to herself, had never caused any trouble and had never attended any parties. A "goody-goody," many had called her. Daniel remembered feeling sorry for her, a sweetheart targeted by the town bully.

Today, his reaction to her endearing shyness and unintentional insults had shocked him. Somehow she'd turned him on so fiercely, he'd felt as if *years* had passed since he'd last had sex rather than a few hours. But then, everything about his most recent encounter with Dot—Dorothea had shocked him.

Upon returning from his morning run, he'd stood in the doorway of his room, watching her work. As she'd vacuumed, she'd wiggled her hips, dancing to music with a different beat than the song playing on his iPod.

Control had been beyond him—he'd hardened instantly.

He'd noticed her appeal on several other occasions, of course. How could he not? Her eyes, once too big for her face, were now a perfect fit and the most amazing shade of green. Like shamrocks or lucky charms, framed by the thickest, blackest lashes he'd ever seen. Those eyes were an absolute show-stopper. Her lips were plump and heart shaped, a fantasy made flesh. And her body...

Daniel grinned up at the ceiling. He suspected she had serious curves underneath her scrubs. The way the material had tightened over her chest when she'd moved...the lushness of her ass when she'd bent over...every time he'd looked at her, he'd sworn he'd developed early-onset arrhythmia.

With her eyes, lips and corkscrew curls, she reminded him of a living doll. *Blow her up, and she'll blow me.* He really wanted to play with her.

But he wouldn't. Ever. She lived right here in town.

When Daniel first struck up a friendship with

Jessie Kay, his father expressed hope for a Christmas wedding and grandkids soon after. The moment Daniel had broken the news—no wedding, no kids—Virgil teared up.

Lesson learned. When it came to Strawberry Valley girls, Virgil would always think long-term, and he would always be disappointed when the relationship ended. Stress wasn't good for his ticker. Daniel loved the old grump with every fiber of his being, wanted him around as long as possible.

Came back to care for him. Not going to make things worse.

Bang, bang, bang!

Daniel palmed his semiautomatic and plunged to the floor to use the bed as a shield. As a bead of sweat rolled into his eye, his finger twitched on the trigger. The screams in his head were drowned out by the sound of his thundering heartbeat.

Bang, bang!

He muttered a curse. The door. Someone was knocking on the door.

Disgusted with himself, he glanced at the clock on the nightstand—1:08 a.m.

As he stood, his dog tags clinked against his mother's locket, the one he'd worn since her death. He pulled on the wrinkled, ripped jeans he'd tossed earlier and anchored his gun against his lower back.

Forgoing the peephole, he looked through the crack in the window curtains. His gaze landed on a dark, wild mass of corkscrew curls, and his frown deepened. Only one woman in town had hair like that, every strand made for tangling in a man's fists.

Concern overshadowed a fresh surge of desire as he threw open the door. Hinges squeaked, and Dorothea paled. But a fragrant cloud of lavender enveloped him, and his head fogged; desire suddenly overshadowed concern.

Down, boy.

She met his gaze for a split second, then ducked her head and wrung her hands. Before, freckles had covered her face. Now a thick layer of makeup hid them. Unfortunate. He liked those freckles, often imagined—

Nothing.

"Is something wrong?" On alert, he scanned left…right… The hallway was empty, no signs of danger.

As many times as he'd stayed at the inn, Dorothea had only ever spoken to him while cleaning his room. Which had always prompted his early-morning departures. There'd been no reason to grapple with temptation.

"I'm fine," she said, and gulped. Her shallow inhalations came a little too quickly, and her cheeks grew chalk white. "Super fine."

How was her tone shrill and breathy at the same time?

He relaxed his battle stance, though his confusion remained. "Why are you here?"

"I…uh… Do you need more towels?"

"Towels?" His gaze roamed over the rest of her, as if drawn by an invisible force—disappointment struck. She wore a bulky, ankle-length raincoat, hiding the body underneath. Had a storm rolled in? He listened but heard no claps of thunder. "No, thank you. I'm good."

"Okay." She licked her porn-star lips and toyed with the tie around her waist. "Yes, I'll have coffee with you."

Coffee? "Now?"

A defiant nod, those corkscrew curls bouncing.

He barked out a laugh, surprised, amazed and delighted by her all over again. "What's really going on, Dorothea?"

Her eyes widened. "My name. You remembered this time." When he stared at her, expectant, she cleared her throat. "Right. The reason I'm here. I just… I wanted to talk to you." The color returned to her cheeks, a sexy blush spilling over her skin. "May I come in? Please. Before someone sees me."

Mistake. That blush gave a man ideas.

Besides, what could Miss Mathis have to say to him? He ran through a mental checklist of possible problems. His bill—nope, already paid in full. His father's health—nope, Daniel would have been called directly.

If he wanted answers, he'd have to deal with Dorothea…alone…with a bed nearby…

Swallowing a curse, he stepped aside.

She rushed past him as if her feet were on fire, the scent of lavender strengthening. His mouth watered.

I could eat her up.

But he wouldn't. Wouldn't even take a nibble.

"Shut the door. Please," she said, a tremor in her voice.

He hesitated but ultimately obeyed. "Would you like a beer while the coffee brews?"

"Yes, please." She spotted the six-pack he'd brought with him, claimed one of the bottles and popped the cap.

He watched with fascination as she drained the contents.

She wiped her mouth with the back of her wrist and belched softly into her fist. "Thanks. I needed that."

He tried not to smile as he grabbed the pot. "Let's get you that coffee."

"No worries. I'm not thirsty." She placed the empty bottle on the dresser. Her gaze darted around the room, a little wild, a lot nervous. She began to pace in front of him. She wasn't wearing shoes, revealing toenails painted yellow and orange, like her fingernails.

More curious by the second, he eased onto the edge of the bed. "Tell me what's going on."

"All right." Her tongue slipped over her lips, moistening both the upper and lower, and the fly of his jeans tightened. In an effort to keep his hands to himself, he fisted the comforter. "I can't really tell you. I have to show you."

"Show me, then." *And leave.* She had to leave. Soon.

"Yes," she croaked. Her trembling worsened as she untied the raincoat…

The material fell to the floor.

Daniel's heart stopped beating. His brain short-circuited. Dorothea Mathis was gloriously, wonderfully naked; she had more curves than he'd suspected, generous curves, *gorgeous* curves.

Was he drooling? He might be drooling.

She wasn't a living doll, he decided, but a 1950s' pinup. *Lord save me.* She had the kind of body other women abhorred but men adored. *He* adored. A vine with thorns and holly was etched around the outside of one breast, ending in a pink bloom just over her heart.

Sweet Dorothea Mathis had a tattoo. He wanted to touch. He *needed* to touch.

A moment of rational thought intruded. Strawberry Valley girls were off-limits…his dad…disappointment… But…

Dorothea's soft, lush curves *deserved* to be touched. Though makeup still hid the freckles on her face, the sweet little dots covered the rest of her alabaster skin. A treasure map for his tongue.

I'll start up top and work my way down. Slowly.

She had a handful of scars on her abdomen and thighs, beautiful badges of strength and survival. More paths for his tongue to follow.

As he studied her, drinking her in, one of her arms draped over her breasts, shielding them from his view. With her free hand, she covered the apex of her thighs, and no shit, he almost whimpered. Such bounty should *never* be covered.

"I want…to sleep with you," she stammered. "One time. Only one time. Afterward, I don't want to speak with you about it. Or about anything. We'll avoid each other for the rest of our lives."

One night of no-strings sex? Yes, please. He wanted her. Here. Now.

For hours and hours…

No. No, no, no. If he slept with the only maid at the only inn in town, he'd have to stay in the city with all future dates, over an hour away from his dad. What if Virgil had another heart attack?

Daniel leaped off the bed to swipe up the raincoat. A darker blush stained Dorothea's cheeks…and spread…and though he wanted to watch the color deepen, he fit the material around her shoulders.

"You…you don't want me." Horror contorted her features as she spun and raced to the door.

His reflexes were well honed; they had to be. They were the only reason he hadn't come home from his tours of duty in a box. Before she could exit, he raced behind her and flattened his hands on the door frame to cage her in.

"Don't run," he croaked. "I like the chase."

Tremors rubbed her against him. "So…you want me?"

Do. Not. Answer. "I'm in a state of shock." And awe. He battled an insane urge to trace his nose along

her nape…to inhale the lavender scent of her skin…
to taste every inch of her. The heat she projected
stroked him, sensitizing already-desperate nerve
endings.

The mask of humanity he'd managed to don before
reentering society began to chip.

Off-kilter, he backed away from her. She remained
in place, clutching the lapels of her coat.

"Look at me," Daniel commanded softly.

After an eternity-long hesitation, she turned. Her
gaze remained on his feet. Which was probably a
good thing. Those shamrock eyes might have been
his undoing.

"Why me, Dorothea?" She'd shown no interest in
him before. "Why now?"

She chewed on her bottom lip and said, "Right
now I don't really know. You talk too much."

Most people complained he didn't talk enough.
But then, Dorothea wasn't here to get to know him.
And he wasn't upset about that—really. He hadn't
wanted to get to know any of his recent dates.

"You didn't answer my questions," he said.

"So?" The coat gaped just enough to reveal a swell
of delectable cleavage as she shifted from one foot to
the other. "Are we going to do this or not?"

Yes!

No! Momentary pleasure, lifelong complications.
"I—"

"Oh, my gosh. You actually hesitated," she squeaked.

"There's a naked girl right in front of you, and you have to think about sleeping with her."

"You aren't my usual type." A Strawberry Valley girl equaled marriage. No ifs, ands or buts about it. The only other option was hurting his dad, so it wasn't an option at all.

She flinched, clearly misunderstanding him.

"I prefer city girls, the ones I have to chase," he added. Which only made her flinch again.

Okay, she hadn't short-circuited his brain; she'd liquefied it. Those curves…

Tears welled in her eyes, clinging to her wealth of black lashes—gutting him. When Harlow Glass had tortured Dorothea in the school hallways, her cheeks had burned bright red but her eyes had remained dry.

I hurt her worse than a bully.

"Dorothea," he said, stepping toward her.

"No!" She held out her arm to ward him off. "I'm not stick thin or sophisticated. I'm too easy, and you're not into pity screwing. Trust me, I get it." She spun once more, tore open the door and rushed into the hall.

This time, he let her go. His senses devolved into hunt mode, as he'd expected, the compulsion to go after her nearly overwhelming him. *Resist!*

What if, when he caught her—and he *would*—he didn't carry her back to his room but took what she'd offered, wherever they happened to be?

Biting his tongue until he tasted blood, he kicked the door shut.

Silence greeted him. He waited for the past to resurface, but thoughts of Dorothea drowned out the screams. Her little pink nipples had puckered in the cold, eager for his mouth. A dark thatch of curls had shielded the portal to paradise. Her legs had been toned but soft, long enough to wrap around him and strong enough to hold on to him until the end of the ride.

Excitement lingered, growing more powerful by the second, and curiosity held him in a vise grip. The Dorothea he knew would never show up at a man's door naked, requesting sex.

Maybe he didn't actually know her. Maybe he should learn more about her. The more he learned, the less intrigued he'd be. He could forget this night had ever happened.

He snatched his cell from the nightstand and dialed Jude, LPH's tech expert.

Jude answered after the first ring, proving he hadn't been sleeping, either. "What?"

Good ole Jude. His friend had no tolerance for bull, or pleasantries. "Brusque" had become his only setting. And Daniel understood. Jude had lost the bottom half of his left leg in battle. A major blow, no doubt about it. But the worst was yet to come. During his recovery, his wife and twin daughters were killed by a drunk driver.

The loss of his leg had devastated him. The loss of his family had changed him. He no longer laughed or smiled; he was like Daniel, only much worse.

"Do me a favor and find out everything you can about Dorothea Mathis. She's a Strawberry Valley resident. Works at the Strawberry Inn."

The faint *click-clack* of typing registered, as if the guy had already been seated in front of his wall of computers. "Who's the client, and how soon does he—she?—want the report?"

"I'm the client, and I'd like the report ASAP."

The typing stopped. "So this is personal," Jude said with no inflection of emotion. "That's new."

"Extenuating circumstances," he muttered.

"She do you wrong?"

I'm not stick thin or sophisticated. I'm too easy, and you're not into pity screwing. Trust me, I get it.

"The opposite," he said.

Another pause. "Do you want to know the names of the men she's slept with? Or just a list of any criminal acts she might have committed?"

He snorted. "If she's gotten a parking ticket, I'll be shocked."

"So she's a good girl."

"I don't know what she is," he admitted. Those corkscrew curls...pure innocence. Those heart-shaped lips...pure decadence. Those soft curves...*mine, all mine.*

"Tell Brock this is a hands-off situation," he said before the words had time to process.

What the hell was wrong with him?

Brock was the privileged rich boy who'd grown up ignored by his parents. He was covered in tats and piercings and tended to avoid girls who reminded him of the debutantes he'd been expected to marry. He preferred the wild ones...those willing to proposition a man.

"Warning received," Jude said. "Dorothea Mathis belongs to you."

He ground his teeth in irritation. "You are seriously irritating, you know that?"

"Yes, and that's one of my better qualities."

"Just get me the details." Those lips...those curves... "And make it fast."

CAN'T HARDLY BREATHE—available soon from Gena Showalter and HQN Books!

COMING NEXT MONTH FROM

HARLEQUIN

Desire

Available October 3, 2017

#2545 BILLIONAIRE BOSS, HOLIDAY BABY
Billionaires and Babies • by Janice Maynard
It's almost Christmas when Dani is snowed in with her too-sexy boss—
and an abandoned baby wearing a note that says he's the father!
Nathaniel needs Dani's help, but playing house means finally facing the
desire they can no longer deny...

#2546 BILLIONAIRE'S BABY BIND
Texas Cattleman's Club: Blackmail • by Katherine Garbera
Amberley knows better than to fall for another city boy, but widowed
tech wizard Will has an infant daughter who makes her heart melt!
When the chemistry between Amberley and Will won't quit, will he open
his heart once more to love?

#2547 LITTLE SECRETS: SECRETLY PREGNANT
by Andrea Laurence
Cautious Emma cut loose once—*once*—at a party, only to find herself
pregnant by her masked lover. She meets him again in the last place
she expects...at work! He's the rebellious CEO of the company she's
auditing. Now can she avoid mixing business with pleasure?

#2548 FIANCÉ IN NAME ONLY
by Maureen Child
Brooding celebrity writer Micah only wants to be alone with his work.
But somehow his gorgeous neighbor has tempted him into the role of
fake fiancé! Now pretend emotions are becoming real desire. So what
happens when their time together comes to an end?

#2549 THE COWBOY'S CHRISTMAS PROPOSITION
Red Dirt Royalty • by Silver James
Quincy Kincaid's vacation is almost within reach, until a baby is
abandoned with a country superstar! She has every intention of
resisting the sexy singer—until they're trapped together for the holidays.
Now all she wants for Christmas is him...

#2550 ONE NIGHT STAND BRIDE
In Name Only • by Kat Cantrell
Playboy Hendrix Harris never calls a woman twice. But after the scandal
of a public Vegas hookup, the only solution is to settle down—with a
convenient marriage. But Roz makes him want more than temporary...
So how will he let her go?

———————

HDCNM0917

Get 2 Free Books,

Plus 2 Free Gifts—

just for trying the Reader Service!

It's almost Christmas when Dani is snowed in with her too-sexy boss—and an abandoned baby wearing a note that says he's the father! Nathaniel needs Dani's help, but playing house means finally facing the desire they can no longer deny…

Read on for a sneak peek of
BILLIONAIRE BOSS, HOLIDAY BABY
by USA TODAY *bestselling author Janice Maynard,*
part of Harlequin Desire's #1 bestselling
***BILLIONAIRES AND BABIES** series.*

This was a hell of a time to feel arousal tighten his body.

Dani looked better than any woman should while negotiating the purchase of infant necessities during the beginnings of a blizzard with her brain-dead boss and an unknown baby.

Her body was curvy and intensely feminine. The clothing she wore to work was always appropriate, but even so, Nathaniel had found himself wondering if Dani was as prim and proper as her office persona would suggest.

Her wide-set blue eyes and high cheekbones reminded him of a princess he remembered from a childhood storybook. The princess's hair was blond. Dani's was more of a streaky caramel. She'd worn it up today in a sexy knot, presumably because of the Christmas party.

While he stood in line, mute, Dani fussed over the contents of the cart. "If the baby wakes up," she said, "I'll hold her. It will be fine."

In that moment, Nathaniel realized he relied on her far more than he knew and for a variety of complex reasons he was loath to analyze.

Clearing his throat, he fished out his wallet and handed the cashier his credit card. Then their luck ran out. The baby woke up and her screams threatened to peel paint off the walls.

Dani's smile faltered, but she unfastened the straps of the carrier and lifted the baby out carefully. "I'm so sorry, sweetheart. Do you have a wet diaper? Let's take care of that."

The clerk pointed out a unisex bathroom, complete with changing station. The tiny room was little bigger than a closet. They both pressed inside.

They were so close he could smell the faint, tantalizing scent of her perfume.

Was it weird that being this close to Dani turned him on? Her warmth, her femininity. Hell, even the competent way she handled the baby made him want her.

That was the problem with blurring the lines between business and his personal life.

Don't miss
BILLIONAIRE BOSS, HOLIDAY BABY
by USA TODAY *bestselling author Janice Maynard,*
available October 2017 wherever
Harlequin® Desire books and ebooks are sold.

www.Harlequin.com

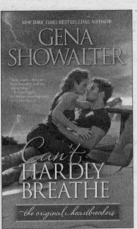

$7.99 U.S./$9.99 CAN.

EXCLUSIVE
Limited Time Offer

$1.⁰⁰ OFF

New York Times Bestselling Author
GENA SHOWALTER
returns with an irresistible
Original Heartbreakers story!

Can't
HARDLY
BREATHE

Available August 29, 2017.
Pick up your copy today!

H
HQN™

$1.⁰⁰
OFF

the purchase price of CAN'T HARDLY BREATHE
by Gena Showalter.

Offer valid from August 29, 2017, to September 30, 2017.
Redeemable at participating retail outlets. Not redeemable at Barnes & Noble.
Limit one coupon per purchase. Valid in the U.S.A. and Canada only.

52615027

5 65373 00076 2   (8100)0 12299

® and ™ are trademarks owned and used by the trademark owner and/or its licensee.

© 2017 Harlequin Enterprises Limited

PHCOUPGSHD0917

LOVE
Harlequin
romance?

Join our Harlequin community to share your thoughts and connect with other romance readers!

Be the first to find out about promotions, news, and exclusive content!

Sign up for the Harlequin e-newsletter and download a free book from any series at

www.TryHarlequin.com

CONNECT WITH US AT:

Harlequin.com/Community

 Facebook.com/HarlequinBooks

 Twitter.com/HarlequinBooks

 Instagram.com/HarlequinBooks

 Pinterest.com/HarlequinBooks

ReaderService.com

**ROMANCE WHEN
YOU NEED IT**

Want to give in to temptation with
steamy tales of irresistible desire?

Check out **Harlequin® Presents®,
Harlequin® Desire** and
Harlequin® Kimani™ Romance books!

New books available every month!

CONNECT WITH US AT:

Harlequin.com/Community

 Facebook.com/HarlequinBooks

 Twitter.com/HarlequinBooks

 Instagram.com/HarlequinBooks

 Pinterest.com/HarlequinBooks

ReaderService.com

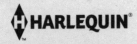 **HARLEQUIN®**

**ROMANCE WHEN
YOU NEED IT**

PGENRE2017